Geraldine crossed  shifted her weight to one hip. "No more secrets. You either tell me exactly what is going on or I fire the girl."

He flushed bright red. A vein throbbed in his forehead. "I can't tell you anything. I made a promise. You, of all people, know I keep my promises." When he spoke, he trembled. "And you can't fire her because I'll just hire her back."

Every molecule of her body tensed. How dare he be more concerned about the girl? She ground her teeth. "Your loyalty belongs to me and not her, understand?"

"No, the problem is *you* don't understand." Scowling, he pointed a thick finger toward her chest. "This situation has nothing to do with you. I will not tolerate your meddling. Leave us alone."

With a sharp intake of air, she squared her shoulders. "Are you having an affair?"

He threw up his arms and tossed back his head. "How can I possibly be having an affair when I can't even make love to my wife?"

Praise for Angela Lam

"Prepare to be captivated by this sweet, page-turning novella [*LOVE AGAIN*] of learning to overcome grief and discovering how to love again. Angela Lam flawlessly executes a gorgeous plot that had me hooked from page one and reading nonstop."

~*C. Rosen*

~*~

"The author has skillfully crafted an utterly addictive and explosive story of trust, second love, and fortitude, mixed with a splash of an indelible commitment between an indigenous American widow and a billionaire with a heart. You won't be able to put it down until you've learned to *LOVE AGAIN*."

~*Jerry Aylward, author*

~*~

"A realistic, thoughtful portrayal of a mature marriage at a crossroads."

~*Liz Crowe, Amazon Best Selling, Award-Winning author of* What Happens in Chicago

~*~

"If you love characters you can really cheer for, read Angela Lam's *NOW AND FOREVER*."

~*Alice Gaines, USA Today bestselling author*

~*~

"A richly emotional tale of what it takes to keep later-in-life romance on track. With equal parts honesty, heart, and depth, Angela Lam weaves a story to remind us that love is all we really ever need."

~*Karen Booth, author*

Now and Forever

by

Angela Lam

Women of the Crush, Book 2

Now and Forever

Cover Art by *Diana Carlile*

The Wild Rose Press, Inc.
PO Box 708
Adams Basin, NY 14410-0708
Visit us at www.thewildrosepress.com

Publishing History
First Edition, 2022
Trade Paperback ISBN 978-1-5092-4308-2
Digital ISBN 978-1-5092-4309-9

Women of the Crush, Book 2
Published in the United States of America

Dedication

For Gina's inspiration and for Kevin's love

"And suddenly we see that love costs all we are, and will ever be."

-Maya Angelou

Chapter One

"I don't believe it." Fifty-two-year-old Geraldine Jones collapsed onto the worn cushion of the swivel chair and restarted the surveillance tape. The red digital clock illuminated ten-thirty, and a faint yellow glow from the streetlight pulsed against the closed blinds in her home office where she reconciled the deli's books on the weekends she didn't want to visit the store. With an elbow propped on the oak table and her chin cupped in her sweaty palm, she slipped reading glasses over the long bridge of her nose and studied the apparitions moving around the loading dock behind Larry's Deli in the small tourist town of Vine Valley, California, two hours north of San Francisco.

Her husband, Lionel, stood with his hands on his waist before the new hire, Michelle "Fair Weather" Wade, an eighteen-year-old girl from the Wapi Reservation.

She lifted her arms, circling them overhead before dropping them and shaking her long black hair.

Geraldine leaned closer. That girl was always dramatic.

He stepped closer and placed his hands on her shoulders.

Good ol' Lionel always calmed down people. That's one of the many things Geraldine loved about him. He was her rock.

Michelle covered her hands over her face and bowed her head.

He slid his hands down the sides of her body and tugged her close.

An uneasy sensation churned in Geraldine's stomach.

Michelle collapsed against his chest.

He stroked her back and kissed her forehead.

Geraldine tapped the pause button on the tape and leaned back against the chair, listening to her jagged breath catch in her throat. After more than thirty-four years together, she never suspected Lionel of cheating. But the tenderness of his hands on Michelle's young body triggered memories of witnessing her father caressing his younger lover in the store room of Larry's Deli. She was only seventeen when she opened the door to retrieve some canned kidney beans Mrs. Gaston needed for her famous Vine Valley chili.

"Don't tell your mother," her father said later, after his mistress left through the loading dock.

Geraldine squeezed her hands into fists, wishing she had struck her father like she wanted to strike Lionel. Maybe she was overreacting. Oh, how she wished she could have heard what was said.

Sighing, she touched the play button to view the rest of the scene.

After rocking her back and forth in his arms, Lionel finally released Michelle. Together, they strolled out of camera range, his large hand on the small of her back.

When the screen faded to black, Geraldine jumped up, knocking the back of the chair against the window, rattling the blinds, and waking the old dog lying by her feet. "C'mon, Noelle, let's go to bed." She patted the side of her leg, smiling at the dog's droopy black eyes.

Downstairs, the garage door click-clacked against the tracks, and the rumble of a truck's engine roared into the space beneath her feet.

Noelle lifted her head and tilted her ears forward.

"Yes, you ol' girl, you heard right. Your daddy is home." Geraldine bent to scratch between Noelle's ears. "Let's go." With Noelle beside her, she descended the staircase one step at a time. The old dog limped, and she wondered how much longer they could keep the home they inherited from Geraldine's father before retiring to a single-level condo closer to downtown.

At the foot of the staircase, she averted her gaze from the hall mirror. She didn't want to glimpse the sunrays of wrinkles radiating from the corners of her faded blue eyes, laugh lines framing her thin mouth like parentheses, and creases of skin lining her neck like the rings on a tree trunk. Getting older was worse than a pet peeve or a distraction. Each year that passed etched another reminder on her body about how far away she was from youth.

Sighing, she straightened the spaghetti straps of the new silk negligee she purchased on her lunch hour after the sales clerk, a young man in his twenties, winked as she held the lingerie against the swell of her small breasts to the length of her long legs in the showroom mirror.

"You're a sexy cougar," he growled.

The sound of his guttural yearning stirred an inkling of desire deep below her belly. She hoped Lionel would notice and react with the same ardent urgency of the sales clerk instead of being lured into the arms of sleep. Stepping into the kitchen, she flicked on the light.

After opening the garage door, Lionel strode into the room.

He smelled of sweat and onions and raw meat from working all day. He set his baseball cap on the tile counter and rubbed thick fingers through his long, white mane of hair. "I'm taking a shower before bed, if you don't mind."

Normally, she wouldn't mind. But tonight, she wanted something different. She wanted to taste the salty bite of his skin and breathe in the scent of his sweat, hoping to catch the telltale whiff of seduction or the stench of backbreaking labor.

Noelle yelped, lifting her paws onto his calves.

He chuckled, rubbing his fingers under her chin. "You good ol' girl."

As soon as Noelle drifted away, Geraldine sashayed to Lionel and wrapped her arms around his shoulders. "Hey, sugar." She winked and drew him against the smooth lingerie.

He flinched. "I'm tired, and you need your beauty sleep." He sloughed off her arms from around his neck and lumbered out of the room.

His rejection clawed into her skin, leaving a gouge of pain. "I saw you and Michelle on the surveillance camera." She crossed her arms over her chest and shifted her weight to one hip. "Why was she crying?"

Pausing beneath the threshold, he glanced over his shoulder. "Just personal stuff."

She steeled her spine. "Why won't you tell me?"

Sighing, he shook his head. "She swore me to secrecy."

"I'm your wife." She knocked her fist against her chest. "You won't break your promise by telling me."

He chuckled. "You're the biggest gossip in Vine Valley."

"What's that comment supposed to mean?" Frowning, she broadened her stance.

After turning to face her squarely, he placed his hands on his hips and narrowed his gaze. "You know exactly what I mean, GG."

Over the years, he had shortened her high school nickname of Golden Goddess to the first two initials. Sighing, she dropped her arms to the sides. The spaghetti straps on the lingerie slid down her shoulders, exposing more skin than the skimpy outfit already supplied. Sure, she liked to talk about the people she knew, but she never spread lies about anyone. "I'm just concerned." She swallowed the rest of the sentence before she could finish—*about you having an affair*.

"Well, concern yourself with something else." He huffed before stomping up the stairs.

Listening to his heavy footfalls, she shoved the spaghetti straps over her shoulders. She hated that young sales clerk for seducing her into a wasteful purchase. Knotting her hands into fists, she wondered if her husband would ever again find her attractive.

Chapter Two

The evening light streaked through the beveled glass door of the Belvedere Bar and fell against Lionel's hands, highlighting the age spots and wrinkles. Extra weight around his middle and arthritis in his spine from unloading boxes of canned goods for over thirty years took a toll on his performance on the softball field. He tipped back the glass and sipped a mouthful of sour-smelling, bitter-tasting beer. A bank of TVs played the local baseball game, but he wasn't paying attention. A bunch of ceiling fans whirred overhead, pushing around cold air. Sweat plastered his long, white hair against the back of his damp neck.

After a crappy senior softball game where he struck out once and walked twice, things couldn't get worse. He had already paid for the first round of beers for his teammates. For those players who wanted to stay, he offered to pay for a second round. Almost all of the guys declined, citing hot dinners with happy families. Only Cassidy Burke, who had the night off from caring for his disabled adult son, and Nick Gold, Jr., who had the luxury to do whatever he wanted, chose to linger.

"What's wrong with your game, Pops?" Laughing, Nick slapped Lionel on the shoulder. "You couldn't hit for shit."

Lionel grumbled. "Everything's just peachy." The

sarcastic bite to his words lingered long after he sipped the bitter brew. As the cold liquid slid down his throat and warmed his stomach, he closed his eyes. Night after night, he kept seeing Geraldine's disappointed face. Failure haunted him. If only he could find something to rejuvenate his male parts, then maybe he could again satisfy his wife's needs.

Crossing his arms on the bar, Cassidy cocked his head to the side. A sandy curl dangled above his hazel eyes. "Uh-oh, sounds like trouble in paradise."

A snicker escaped from Lionel's lips. Cassidy was a general contractor who built the best buildings and a published poet with heightened sensitivity that earned him the name of Romeo on the softball field. He was also an expert on marriage difficulties. Shortly after his twentieth wedding anniversary, he initiated a relationship with his high school sweetheart, a Carmelite nun. The affair ended with his wife divorcing him and his girlfriend leaving the convent. Even though Cassidy married the former nun, the trajectory of their relationship left Lionel skeptical. "Just drink your beer and mind your business."

Nick waved to the bartender for another round. "This one's on me."

Narrowing his eyes, Lionel rapped his fingertips on the counter. Nick was the youngest on the team, having just turned fifty-one in the spring, and he was the only one of the bunch rich enough to retire. Having spent most of his life as a good-looking bachelor and the son of the man who built Vine Valley, he recently wed a Native American widow, Hope "Spirit Walk" Spencer, after helping her save her deceased husband's art gallery. Not only was Nick "Billionaire Boy" dashingly handsome with a full head of dark hair and grayed temples, he was also the best player on the team. "You shouldn't pay for anything. You hit three home runs."

"Well, I'm hoping one more beer might cheer you up." Nick leaned closer. "Work problems?"

A knot of tension loosened across Lionel's upper back. "Work's easy. Everything else is complicated." He cupped the fresh mug of beer.

Cassidy lifted his chin. "Home problems?"

Sighing, Lionel bowed his head. Why not confess? He trusted these guys, no matter what their flaws. "The ship doesn't set sail anymore."

"Have you tried any drugs?" Nick dropped his hand from the mug, leaned closer, and focused his gaze.

Lionel nodded. "All of them. Sure, they work, but they make me feel bad afterward." He ran his hands up and down the moist glass. "What's the point if I feel worse?"

Cassidy shook his head. "I guess I'm lucky. I don't have that problem."

Nick laughed. "You married a virgin. If you couldn't perform, she wouldn't know what she was missing." He slapped a hand on the counter. "Lionel's been with the same woman forever. She expects a certain level of care, if you know what I mean."

"Oh, I know what you mean." Lionel tipped the glass and swallowed a mouthful of cold beer. "Geraldine's great, but her engine's revving to go while mine's barely idling." He pursed his lips. "Sometimes I worry she'll get too disappointed and leave me."

Cassidy scrunched his face and slapped Lionel's shoulder. "Don't talk like that. You guys are glue."

Groaning, Lionel shook his head. Oh, why couldn't

he feel that rush of blood flooding his extremities without the pounding headaches or the raw edge of uncomfortable heat beneath his skin? He bit the inside of his lower lip, determined not to let the emotion well up. "Every night when I get home and she's all dolled up, I feel like a failure because my body won't respond like it used to." He took a sip and set the half-empty mug on the counter. "I just don't know what to do."

"Have you tried any natural remedies?" Nick asked. "Hope might know of something."

Tipping back his head, Lionel chuckled. "I don't need your witchy woman working any hocus-pocus."

Frowning, Nick shifted on the bar stool. "I'll ask. She won't mind helping."

"You keep forgetting she's friends with my wife. I don't want Geraldine to know I've confided in you about my problem." Heat prickled his face. He hadn't even talked to her about it. Not properly. She only knew he hadn't renewed his prescriptions.

"Hope's discreet." Cassidy arched an eyebrow. "No one knew she was dating Nick until after he proposed."

Cassidy was right. Not even Geraldine suspected. Lionel swallowed another mouthful of beer. "Is Hope still affiliated with the tribe?" He eyed Nick.

"She's their new medicine woman. Her cousin, Wayne, recently retired." Nick crinkled his forehead. "Why?"

"I think I should talk with her." Not necessarily about his impotence, but about one of his employees who needed some assistance he wasn't quite sure how to give. Ordinarily, he would have asked Geraldine, but he decided to keep his mouth shut after she bombarded him with questions. Guilt rubbed inside him like a pebble at the bottom of a shoe, making his whole body uncomfortable. He stooped over his beer mug. How long could he keep a secret?

"Here's her number." Nick flashed the contact information on his phone.

With his fat fingers, Lionel typed her name and number as a contact in his phone.

"Do you want Deb to talk to Geraldine?" Cassidy scratched the sandy stubble on his chin. "She could tell her there are more important things to a relationship than sex."

"Let's leave Geraldine out of things for now." Lionel tipped back the mug and finished the beer. After slapping his hands on the counter, he stood. He didn't like feeling helpless in front of his teammates, especially since he was their captain. Leaders didn't need help; they offered it. That's how he functioned. "Thanks for the drink, Nick. I'm calling it a night. I have to face the music sooner or later."

Nick nudged his arm. "No problem."

"Tell Geraldine we said hello." Cassidy slid over to Lionel's stool.

"You guys don't drink too much or stay too late." Lionel snatched his baseball cap off the counter. When he nudged against the beveled glass door, he squinted at the setting sun blazing against the horizon. Even the day ended. So, why shouldn't his love life end?

Chapter Three

Standing behind the deli counter, Geraldine could see the entire store—every aisle and every person. Usually she was adept at keeping watch while making sandwiches, often toggling back and forth between her bird's-eye view and her customer's attention.

Two pieces of crisp sourdough bread sprung from the toaster, and she grabbed the warm slices and placed them on the counter.

From the back of the store, Lionel wheeled a dolly full of cardboard boxes to aisle five.

Michelle trailed after him.

Geraldine narrowed her gaze. Why was Lionel helping her? Didn't he know the girl needed to learn responsibility?

"I said, 'no mustard'. "

The customer's voice sliced through her thoughts. Glancing down at the yellow smears, she gasped. "Oh, sugar, I'm sorry." Swiveling, she dumped two more slices of bread in the toaster.

"No problem. Just gives me more time to admire your beauty, pretty lady."

Pretty lady? The compliment powered through her body like a jolt of caffeine. She shifted her focus to the customer. From his closely cropped reddish hair to his twinkling green eyes and freckled skin, she suspected he was younger. Not much younger judging by the lines around his smile. Having never seen him before, she guessed he must be new to town. "What's your name, sugar?"

"Elliot Flynn." Across the counter, he offered a hand. "And you?"

"Geraldine Jones." She discarded the plastic gloves and grasped his hand with a firm shake.

After rubbing her fingers in his palm, he lifted her hand to his lips for a kiss. "What a pleasure to meet you, Miss Geraldine."

"Mrs. Jones." A rush of blood to her hand left her dizzy. She gripped the counter with her other hand, steadying her legs. Oh, why could she feel the impression of his lips against her skin after he released her?

"You're too young to be married." He winked.

After tugging another pair of gloves over her hands, she adjusted the fingers. The skin still tingled from where his lips met the tender flesh. Pivoting toward the toaster, she shied away from the heat invading her face. She grabbed the two slices and laid them on the counter, searching for a fresh knife to spread the mayonnaise. Glancing over Elliot's shoulder, she glimpsed Lionel as he lifted the boxes from the dolly. How many times did she have to remind him to stop treating all the young hires like children? Didn't he know Michelle was a vibrant young woman who could probably lift more than he could carry? She swallowed a sudden tightness in her throat. Her father had treated employees the same way, coddling them, especially the women. With a sudden intake of air, she returned her gaze to the sandwich. Deep down in her bones, she suspected something was wrong, but she couldn't pinpoint exactly what it was.

Elliot followed her gaze. "That your husband?"

She nodded. "Lionel and I own the store."

"I'm hoping to close a deal on Jasper's Bar and Grill this week, if I can get the financing."

"Shame the last owners lost the restaurant right after they remodeled." She shook her head, remembering. "I told them to go with Nick for financing, but they chose Herbert instead."

"Who's Nick?" He wrinkled his nose.

She raised an eyebrow, studying him closer. "Sugar, you can't be from around here if you've never heard of Nick Gold, Jr." After removing the plastic gloves, she plunged a hand into her apron pocket where she kept a stack of business cards from all the locals, doling them out to whoever needed them. Spreading the cards like a hand of poker, she plucked out Nick's card and offered it to Elliot. "Call him. He helped refinance this store after my father died. If he can't help you, then you can't be helped." She flashed a smile.

He flipped the card in his hand. "That's awfully nice of you."

She hitched her breath, hypnotized by the delicate way he caressed the card. Swallowing, she wrapped the turkey sandwich in white butcher paper, taped the sides, and scrawled, *Free, GG*, in big, bold black marker. "Welcome to Vine Valley. The sandwich is on me." She waved her manicured nails and widened her smile. "Have a nice day, sugar."

"You, too, pretty lady." He winked before he strolled away.

As soon as he was gone, she wiped her hands on a dish towel and eyed Michelle's progress.

The girl bent her legs, plucked one can from the cardboard box, and stood for a second before arranging the can on the shelf.

Could anyone work any slower?

"May I have a tuna sandwich on white bread?" the next customer asked.

"Of course, you may." Forcing a smile, she glanced at the line of people shifting from foot to foot. Confronting Michelle would have to wait.

Lionel barreled up behind her and washed his hands in the sink. "I'm taking over, GG. You have a delivery to make." He dried his hands on a dish towel and plucked a folded piece of paper from his pocket.

She frowned at the messy print. Why couldn't he learn to slow down when he took a phone message? Slowly, words formed out of the jumbled script. *Two pastrami on rye with everything to 777 Wild Oak Court.* She arched an eyebrow. "That's Cassidy and Deb's house."

Smiling, he nodded. "Don't keep your friends waiting."

After tucking the order into her apron pocket, she grabbed the loaf of rye bread while Lionel helped the next customer. She tingled, remembering the last time she delivered sandwiches to Deb. Her friend had taken a leave of absence from the Carmelite Monastery of Santa Fe, New Mexico, to care for her mother, Laura, who had been diagnosed with lung cancer. That little event led to a gold rush of gossip, as Deb embarked on a secret love affair with Cassidy, which led to his divorce. Shortly after Laura's passing, Deb left the convent and married Cassidy, taking on the role of stepmother to his disabled son, Adam, who functioned more like an overgrown toddler than an adult. Oh, what bit of juicy gossip might land in her lap today?

****

How can time speed and slow simultaneously? Lionel hustled through the sandwich orders—smoked ham and extra sharp cheddar cheese toasted until the cheese melted just right, roast beef and tomato with extra mayo, salami and Monterey Jack on sourdough with everything on it—hoping to finish the lunch rush before Geraldine returned.

A splinter of truth lodged beneath his skin, creating an itch. He needed to talk with Michelle about last week when she cornered him on the loading dock. What did she mean when she said the Great Spirit had told her to trust him?

She had circled her arms to the sky, complaining about her boyfriend, Paul "Fire Walker" Hughes, with whom she lived on the reservation. She spoke like the Wapi River after a flood—a gush of noise without pauses, her words tumbling all over, splattering information everywhere.

From the puddles, he glimpsed a watery story of love and violence. But what worried him the most, besides her plea not to tell anyone, was her speculation she might be pregnant. How could a young woman navigate parenthood when she dwelled in an abusive atmosphere?

By a quarter after one, the line of hungry customers trickled. He finished the last order, washed and dried his hands, and glanced around the store.

Michelle ducked into the back for her lunch break.

A rush of adrenaline spiked in his blood. With clumsy hands, he closed the counter, flipping over the

Be Back in Fifteen Minutes sign, and followed her.

She sat at the round table, rubbing the long sleeves covering her arms, waiting for the microwave to heat her food.

The smells of tarragon and wild onion wafted through the warm room. Lionel motioned to the empty chair. "May I join you?"

She nodded, her hands still traveling the length of the shirt sleeves.

Glancing at the surveillance cameras, he winced.

About a year ago, the trouble had started. As soon as school ended, teenagers loitered in the parking lot, leaving beer cans and used condoms on the pavement.

Geraldine fumed. "We never behaved that way when we were growing up."

He disagreed, reminiscing about the tailgate parties after football games in the high school parking lot. "They're just kids," he told her.

But she insisted on installing a security system.

Eventually, after vandals sprayed *Injun lovers go to hell* beneath the signage and smashed the storefront windows to steal beef jerky and candy bars, he had relented. Sure, the store was safe, but no privacy existed.

Should he go into the office and stop the recording? A knot tightened in his stomach. He didn't know anything about technology.

Geraldine operated the software from their home office.

He hadn't even paid attention when the technician installed the system. Never mind. Learning would take too much time. He folded his hands in his lap to stop the tenderness tugging at the tips of his fingers, urging him to touch Michelle's hunched shoulders. Taking a deep breath, he prepared to talk. At least the camera didn't record voices. A modicum of privacy remained, in spite of the eternal witness. "Are you okay today?"

The timer on the microwave dinged. Michelle stood and retrieved her bowl. With a fork, she tossed the steaming purple and yellow roots over the fragrant rice. Without lifting her face, she nodded.

Muscles bristled along his spine. She was lying. With her downcast eyes and droopy shoulders, she appeared tense and worried. If Geraldine hadn't lost the twins during her pregnancy twenty years ago, he would have had a daughter around Michelle's age. He sighed. That old ache of loss never left. The emptiness echoed like a voice in a hollow, and he filled the space with beer and buddies, instead of confiding in Geraldine who had suffered the same loss. "Have you taken a pregnancy test yet?"

Swallowing, she dropped her fork and raised her eyes. "I can't get one. He never lets me out of his sight." The words caught in her throat. "I don't know where to go."

He placed a hand on her wrist.

Flinching, she tucked her hand into her lap.

He dropped his fingers onto the hard table. If she trusted him, then why did she retreat? He shifted in the chair. "I won't hurt you. I want to help." He didn't know if lowering his voice built confidence or suspicion. "I can buy you a test. You could take it here. He won't know."

She stared at her bowl of untouched food. Her curtain of black hair shielded her face. "What will I do if I am?"

A sharp pain jabbed the back of his throat. "We'll figure out that later. Right now, we just need to know." He withdrew his hand from the table and stood. Glancing at the camera in the corner of the room, he resisted the urge to rip it out of the wall. After shoving his hands into his pockets, he pivoted. "I'll buy one tonight. Come early tomorrow. The test works best first thing in the morning, okay?"

Nodding, she heaved her shoulders. A sob escaped from her pinched lips.

A wave of tenderness washed over him, and he knelt beside her, wrapping his arms around her shuddering shoulders, his mouth beside the long hair that smelled of sage and morning dew. "I'll be here when you find out," he promised. "Whatever the result is, you won't be alone."

Chapter Four

When Geraldine drove up to the white-and-yellow, ranch-style house at the end of the cul-de-sac, she glimpsed Deb sitting on the porch in the gated front yard. She had cut her graying hair short around the ears, her compact body boxy beneath the white T-shirt and denim jeans.

Geraldine parked the car on the street beside the curb, grabbed the sandwiches in a brown paper bag stamped with the logo for Larry's Deli, and sashayed toward the house. The thick summer heat clung to her pores, dampening her skin like a hot flash.

"Thanks for coming." Deb held open the gate and ushered Geraldine into the house. "Let's eat inside."

Stepping into the living room, Geraldine smiled at the personal touches Deb added to the space since moving into the house one year ago. Gone were the knickknacks and clutter that filled the mantel above the fireplace and scattered over the coffee table and end tables. A picture of Cassidy and Deb at their wedding with Adam between them graced the mantel. A new sofa that appeared soft to the touch replaced the old worn leather couch. A ceiling fan whipped a batch of cooler air, and a light scent of pine filled the room.

Deb motioned toward the kitchen. After pulling back a chair for Geraldine, she ambled over to the refrigerator, grabbed a pitcher, and poured two glasses of lemonade.

A leather notebook sat at the far end of the table, a pen laid across the cover. Geraldine removed the sandwiches and napkins. "Have you written any poems lately?"

Taking a seat, Deb shook her head. "That's Cassidy's notebook. He's writing a chapbook of poems in honor of my mother."

Did Deb ask her over to play the muse? Geraldine shoved back her shoulders and tossed her blonde hair over one shoulder. "Oh, sugar, why aren't you writing?"

Deb tipped back her head and laughed. "I'm always writing. I just don't have the same ambitions for publication he does."

All right, then. Geraldine crossed her ankles. What could be the reason for the visit? Glancing around the kitchen nook with its windows overlooking the front yard, she frowned. "Is Cassidy joining us?"

"Not today. He's working with Nick at the old, abandoned warehouse downtown. I thought I'd grab a little girl time before the bus drops off Adam from adult daycare at three." She bowed her head, made the sign of the cross, and silently prayed. When she was finished, she met Geraldine's gaze. "I hope you don't mind."

Widening her eyes, Geraldine lifted her hands and shook her head. "Oh, no, sugar, I don't mind at all." She tucked her hands into her lap, leaned forward, and softened her gaze. Being a sympathetic listener was paramount to being a great gossip. People wanted to confide in someone who was compassionate and eager to help. "Anything you want to talk about?"

Deb swallowed a bite. "How are things with you

and Lionel?"

Geraldine puckered her lips, a sour taste filling her mouth. Why had Deb turned the tables? Geraldine wasn't fodder for gossip. Or was she? Dipping her head, she focused on her untouched sandwich. How many nights had she gone to bed, wishing for a spark to ignite between her and Lionel? Maybe her domestic problems were the next hot topic. Already she could hear the murmurs: GG and LJ have lost the magic touch. Will their love survive? She held her breath, delaying a response. Could she lie to her best friend and get away with it? "We're fine, sugar." She lifted her head and forced her lips into a smile. "What about you and Cassidy?"

Deb took a sip of lemonade. "Actually, he's—how shall I phrase this tactfully?—a little too frisky these days."

A pang squeezed her chest. Why did the virgin get the horny guy? She tightened her smile. "Just fake it 'til you make it, sugar." Over the years, she had purchased several gadgets to manufacture desire. Some worked. Others didn't. "Take a long, hot bath to relax. Then slip on some sexy lingerie and spray some perfume on the insides of your wrists." She picked up her sandwich. "Light some candles and read something naughty to get the juices flowing."

"I don't want to put in all that effort." Deb winced. "Can't I turn him down gently without hurting his ego or damaging our relationship?"

Biting into the toasted rye, crispy lettuce, and salty pastrami, Geraldine pondered Deb's question. Rejection was rejection, no matter how you sliced it. Every night Lionel brushed aside her advances left her feeling cold and discarded like an unwanted newspaper left on the porch. After swallowing a second bite, she rinsed her mouth with tart lemonade. How could she give advice on something she struggled with? She identified with Cassidy's pining for attention, but not Deb's skittering away.

"What do you do when Lionel wants too much affection?" Deb arched an eyebrow.

Dark laughter escaped from her mouth. "Oh, sugar, that situation hasn't happened in so long I can't remember."

"Really?" Deb's mouth fell open, and she leaned closer.

Heat invaded Geraldine's face, and she glanced away. When was the last time Lionel shoved her back against the wall and slipped his tongue into the warm cavern of her mouth, his hands roaming the sides of her curves and igniting every inch of her skin with desire? The gaps in her memory skipped over days, weeks, and months. She bit her lower lip, recalling the prescriptions he tried. Some had worked better than others. All of them left him complaining about either body aches or headaches. One of them ignited a furnace inside him, leaving his skin crawling with unbearable heat. A vial of pills, untouched, remained in his nightstand drawer. How much time had passed since he used one?

"Geraldine?"

The shock of Deb's cool fingers against the back of her hand snapped Geraldine into the present moment. She lifted her head and gazed into her friend's troubled eyes.

"What's wrong?" Deb curled her fingers and squeezed her hand.

"Oh, sugar, don't worry about me." Geraldine tugged free her hand and waved off Deb's concern. Grabbing the glass of lemonade, she took a sip of the sugary liquid. The cool, moist sides of the glass refreshed against her hot, dry skin. She wanted to run the beads of moisture against her forehead, close her eyes, and forget about the tension mounting in her shoulders.

"I've been your best friend since high school. Please, tell me what's going on." Deb rubbed together her thumb and index finger.

That annoying habit mirrored the way Deb worried her rosary beads. Why lie? Deb would only see through it and give her a lecture about honesty. Taking a deep breath, Geraldine sighed. "Lionel and I haven't had sex in months." She grabbed a paper napkin and dabbed at the corners of her eyes. "He stopped taking his prescription because he said he didn't like the side effects."

Deb gasped. "I would have never guessed. You guys are so chummy on the softball field."

Geraldine waved a hand. "If you're known as a flirt, you even flirt with your husband." She crumpled the rough napkin into a ball in her fist. "I don't know how to help you, because I don't know how you feel." She sniffed. "I identify with Cassidy—all hot and bothered with nowhere to go." Another thought flitted through her mind. "I never imagined Lionel might feel bad about the situation, too."

Frowning, Deb cupped the sides of her glass. "Maybe we should switch husbands."

Geraldine laughed. She didn't find the dreamy poet, left-handed pitcher all that attractive. She preferred Lionel with his soft brown eyes, large gentle hands, and low scruffy voice. "Thanks, sugar, but he's not my type."

Nodding, Deb smiled. "I feel that same way about Lionel. He's a nice guy, but not for me."

Geraldine stared at her half-eaten sandwich. She never imagined struggling with something so elemental. Her sex life had gone from a gushing river to a trickling stream to a dry riverbed just as she was getting ready for a long swim. She picked at a piece of pastrami with her manicured nails. Sure, no couple had identical sex drives, but most couples weren't on opposite extremes. She glanced at her friend, who stood on dry sands of the empty river, no longer craving the intimacy of touch, while she perched above the rushing current, eager to dive into the stream of lust. Shaking her head, she sighed. "Oh, sugar, what will we do?"

Chapter Five

Carrying Michelle's secret took root in Lionel. He left work early, asking the assistant manager to stay late and close the store. Driving south out of Vine Valley, he stopped at the first drug store where no one would know his name. He stepped from the lashing afternoon heat into the cool mouth of the building, swallowed into a bigger world of glossy displays and fancy price tags with bar codes. No one stopped to ask if he needed assistance. After reading the signs above the aisles, he located a pregnancy test. Clutching the box to his chest, he strode toward the checkout.

A family stood ahead of him. The mother set her items on the conveyor belt, and the son pointed to the rack of gum. "May I have one?" he asked, widening his eyes.

The mother eyed the gum then her son. With pursed lips, she shook her head. "You didn't clean your room. I'm not rewarding that behavior."

"Please." He clasped his hands against his chest and jumped up and down. "I'll clean it when I get home."

"No." She swiveled, stalking toward the end of the counter.

He scrunched his face and cried.

Raising her eyebrows, she set her purse on the counter and yanked his arm. "Don't make a scene," she hissed. Glancing up, she caught Lionel's gaze. "I'm sorry, sir, if he's disturbed you."

Lionel shook his head, dumbfounded by the interaction. "Would it be all right if I bought him a pack of gum, but you only give it after he cleans his room?"

The woman stepped back, her mouth agape. "You don't need to do that, sir."

"I want to." He stepped forward and patted the boy on his shoulder. "You promise to obey your mother, and I'll pay for your gum, okay?"

The boy nodded.

"Which one do you want?"

After the boy selected a double pack of bubble gum, he handed it to Lionel. "Thank you, sir."

"You're welcome." Lionel flashed a smile and placed the item beside the pregnancy test on the conveyor belt. "Just remember to listen to your mother, okay? She knows what's right for you. That's her job."

The boy nodded again.

After the clerk scanned the gum, Lionel handed it to the woman.

"Thank you, sir." She tucked the gum into her purse. "And good luck." She nodded toward the pregnancy test.

Heat invaded his face. He stood still, his arms dangling. An itch grew at the back of his throat. "Oh, that's not for me." He slumped. "I'm too old to have children."

"Oh, your first grandchild?"

He caught the sparkle in her hazel eyes, and the truth punched his gut. Without children, he would never have grandchildren. Why did he think shopping at another store would prevent the pain from surfacing again? He hated to disappoint this stranger, but he didn't want to lie. "No, it's for a friend who can't get to the store."

She glanced from the pregnancy test to the ring on his left hand, and the light extinguished from her eyes. Frowning, she grabbed her son's hand. "I hope *your friend* gets the result she wants."

The judgment didn't escape him. If he opened his mouth to explain, the words might fracture him. His story was too difficult to understand.

She ushered her son out of the store.

The clerk announced the grand total for the purchase.

After shoving a hand into his pocket, Lionel removed his wallet and set a twenty on the counter. He grabbed his change and the brown paper bag, hoping no one would mistake him for a drunk as he left the store.

****

What a day. The service bell rang from the loading dock. Who could Geraldine send? All of her key employees were engaged with customers. Sighing, she wiped her hands on her apron and hustled to the back of the store. The heat from the warehouse knocked her back, and she punched the red button to roll up the doors of the loading dock. Early evening heat shimmered, and she squinted against the lowering sun.

"Sorry I'm late. There was an accident on the freeway." Cody, the soda delivery guy, swaggered around the truck. "Where shall I place this order?"

She held her breath. My, oh, my, how his bronze arms and legs glistened with sweat. A jolt of lust powered through her. Releasing her breath, she widened her smile. "Over here, sugar." She pointed to the space between boxes of dry goods and the walk-in refrigerator.

Cody lowered the pneumatic lift.

His backside rivaled his front. A sudden urge to wrap her arms around him shot through the length of her body. She stiffened. What was wrong with her? Cody was a decade younger and recently engaged. A sinking feeling plunged into her stomach. Was she becoming her father? Frowning, she shook the thought loose from her mind. "I'll have Jeff sort out the rest of the order." She swiveled on her heels and staggered back into the store.

In her apron pocket, her cell phone pinged. She ducked behind a display of toilet paper and removed her phone. With quivering fingers, she swiped the screen and read the message from Lionel.

—*Home by seven. No cooking tonight. Let's celebrate. I'm feeling frisky.*—

Heat scorched her face. Thank goodness her husband couldn't read her thoughts. After all, Cody was not in need of a little extra spice to his sex life. Quickly, she typed a response.

—*Will be home as soon as possible. Last shipment arrived late.*—

She shoved her phone back into her apron pocket and fanned her face with her hands. She was no better than her father. Only opportunity separated them. He had a chance to live out his fantasies. She did not.

****

Was lighting candles too much? Lionel stepped back from the kitchen table. He plated the lasagna on the silver serving tray they received as a twenty-five-years anniversary gift from Nick and scooped out the garden salad into bowls along with the Italian dressing. In a Wapi Indian basket woven by Hope, he wrapped the warm garlic bread. From the curio cabinet, he removed the wine goblets Cassidy and Deb gave them last Christmas.

During the drive back from the drug store, he remembered the last time they dined out, which was a little over a year ago during a softball tournament in Las Vegas. That night after dinner, they staggered along the strip, the neon lights blotting the moon and stars, the music from the Bellagio accompanying the water show, and crowds of strangers jostling shoulder to shoulder for a view. He held her hand and strode away from the steady stream of people toward their hotel. In the elevator, when he kissed her, she smelled of smoke from the casino.

The scent of cigarettes propelled him back toward memories of high school. They believed they were sophisticated, lighting up after making out beneath the bleachers, until they both coughed so much they drew attention from the coach. They lost the only privacy they had until after college graduation when they got married and moved into the tiny apartment above the store, the same space now used as an office.

The memories triggered a stirring deep in his groin, a sensation that had been missing for months. That feeling propelled him to take the next exit and pull into Lorenzo's parking lot to order a three-course, Italian, takeout meal with a bottle of merlot. With the table decorated like a celebratory feast and the setting sun slanting through the kitchen window like a spotlight, he decided candles might be too much.

The garage door rattled along the tracks, and he

jumped.

Noelle barked from underneath the kitchen table.

With trembling fingers, he dimmed the lights on the chandelier.

Prancing from paw to paw, Noelle skittered on the hardwood floor, her hind legs spreading.

Lionel nudged her back onto the area rug before she collapsed into a heap of fur. Oh, how they were all growing old. Opening the garage door, he glimpsed his wife's haggard face beneath the light in the rafters.

"Smells good." Stepping into the kitchen, she tilted her chin.

"You smell good." The faint scent of gardenias lingered on her skin. He lured her into his arms and kissed her, parting her lips with his tongue.

She gasped, placing a hand against his firm chest.

Warmth flooded his body. Oh, how he hoped the feeling would last.

Noelle barked, nudging her damp nose between them.

Geraldine twisted away, laughing. Bending, she patted the dog's soft, furry head. "We haven't forgotten you, baby."

Grabbing a stick of garlic bread, Lionel broke off a piece and took two steps before setting it in the stainless steel bowl next to the table.

Noelle limped across the rug and dipped her snout, lifting the treasured treat in her jaws. She curled up beneath the table and gnawed on the bread like it was a bone.

Tugging Geraldine back into his arms, Lionel nuzzled his nose against her neck. "I'm feeling frisky," he whispered into her ear. "Let's start with dessert."

"Great idea." She wove her fingers through his hand and led him up the staircase. In the bedroom, she spun, tugging his shirt over his head.

He unbuckled his belt and slid out of his pants.

She threw off her shirt and shimmied out of her slacks.

Pulling her close, he snapped off her bra. Oh, how her smooth, cool skin prickled against his calloused hands. Pressing her back against the mattress, he stepped out of his boxer shorts and wriggled her underwear over her hips. Naked, he lay against her. The passion, which had propelled him forward, instantly reversed.

She stroked him.

"Don't." He rolled off her and seized a pillow against his face, stifling a scream. Oh, how could his body betray him?

"It's okay." She snuggled against his back.

The warmth of her breasts suffused him with agitation. Inching toward the edge of the mattress, he shuddered. "No, it's not." Salt stung his eyes. The distant warmth of her breath against his skin didn't stir anything below the waist. He punched the pillow. What was wrong with him? Why was he suddenly broken? He fumbled in the nightstand. After twisting off the top of a medicine bottle, he sat and stared at the dreaded blue pills. If he took one, or even half of one, he might be able to perform, but he couldn't sleep. His body would feel like a furnace, burning all night, and the blood would pound like a hammer against his skull. He heaved his shoulders.

"Don't take them if they make you feel bad, sugar." She scooted beside him, dangling her legs over the mattress until her feet touched the floor. "You already feel terrible. If you take those things, you'll feel worse. Then I'll feel rotten because you took them for me." She bowed her head and wiggled her toes.

"You're right." Standing, he gathered their clothes and tossed them onto the sheets. "Why don't we eat and try again later?"

Nodding, she hooked her bra and slipped into her underwear.

With sagging shoulders, he buckled his belt and sighed. She deserved someone better than him, someone young enough to still please her. Without a word, he followed her down the stairs into the fading light of the dining room.

The smells of tomato sauce and garlic bread rose as heavy as mist.

Chapter Six

Last night was a complete disaster. Geraldine opened the front door and tossed a treat onto the lawn, enticing Noelle to climb down the two steps of the porch and into the yard. Walking had become such a chore for the old dog that Geraldine wondered how much longer she could climb the stairs to the bedroom without needing to be carried.

Breathing in the chill of the morning fog, she sighed, recalling the events of last night. After the failed attempt at lovemaking, they had eaten a lukewarm dinner in relative silence. The lasagna was too salty. The salad was too limp. The garlic sticks were too stale. Even the tiramisu was nothing more than soggy mush. By the time they cleaned up and walked the dog, they were both too exhausted to try lovemaking again. The only bright spot of the evening was when Lionel shared a story Michelle had told him about the otters floating on the ocean at night holding hands so they wouldn't drift apart during sleep.

"Let's be otters." He grasped her hand.

Noelle stopped and squatted, her hind legs trembling.

Geraldine bent to put the warm poop into a plastic bag. When had her life come down to the dullness of routine?

Oh, sure, Lionel romanced her with a fancy dinner.

But the results made the effort seem worthless. Why try and fail when they could avoid disappointment by not trying at all?

When she woke this morning, she hoped they might attempt to make love again, but Lionel had already left to open the store. She rolled onto her side and stroked his pillow, imagining what would have happened if he had stayed a little longer. By the time she padded downstairs, she found he had left half a pot of coffee and a note by an empty mug. *Sorry about last night.* She smiled and tucked the note into a box of recipes where she also kept the cards he had given her over the years.

After sweetening her coffee with cream and sugar, she stepped onto the deck and lingered over the railing, gazing with wonder at the late-blooming roses that smelled thick with promise. Even Noelle's limp seemed better as she trotted along the planks of the deck, sniffing.

Now, she dumped the poop bag into the garbage can and climbed up the steps of the porch and into the house with Noelle behind her. She rubbed the dog's head until her eyes closed with pleasure, wondering how much longer the despondency would last.

****

Standing like a sentinel outside the employee bathroom, Lionel waited for Michelle to take the pregnancy test. The back door of the loading dock was open, and the foggy breath of early morning exhaled into the room. He crossed his arms over his chest, preventing the warmth from leaving his body, and recalled the romantic dinner beginning with dessert last night. He bowed his head and stared at his feet. Oh, how he hated disappointing GG again.

The lock on the door clicked, and Michelle stepped into the chilly room, holding the white wand as far away from her body as her arm would extend. "It's positive." She shuddered.

Seizing the test from her fingers, he squinted at the two blue lines on the tiny screen. The sight jolted him back twenty years when he stood upstairs in the loft apartment and Geraldine danced around him, waving the white stick like a magic wand. "I'm pregnant," she sang. "We'll celebrate our anniversary with a baby in our new home." He stiffened. The babies never saw the decorated nursery. The babies died before they made it to their home.

Sniffling lured him back to the present. With her arms wrapped around her waist, Michelle tucked her chin to her chest and sobbed.

She appeared to want to curl into a tiny ball and roll away. The test dangled from his fingers, and he glanced around the room, not knowing where to put it. The clock against the wall read six forty-five. By seven, the first employees would arrive to prepare for another busy day.

"What will I do?" She lifted her tear-streaked face, her eyes red and swollen.

With the test in one of his fists, he wrapped his arms around her shoulders and tugged her against his chest. "I don't know, sweetheart." The words rolled off his tongue, and he tightened the embrace. "Depends on what you want." He kissed her hair that smelled of sage. His actions held no chastisement, only the tenderness of a parent toward a child.

She wriggled away. "I don't know how to be a

mother. I didn't have good parents. My mom drank. My dad spent too much time at the casino."

He stiffened. Could he convince her to give up the child for adoption? Maybe he and GG could be foster parents until a permanent family could be found. He heaved a sigh. No, that solution was just a fantasy. Even if she had been his daughter, he couldn't decide for her. But he could offer his support. "I'll help either way."

"Thank you." A faint smile rose on her face.

Some part of him wanted to cradle her like he had cradled Noelle those first few months she was a puppy. But she was a young woman. She was also unwed and pregnant, living on the reservation and working for him. Resisting the impulse to touch her again, he stepped back and waved the stick. "Do you want to keep this thing, or should I dispose of it before the others arrive?"

Frowning, she flicked her wrist. "Get rid of it."

He grabbed the paper bag from the table in the employee break room and buried the test at the bottom.

"Wait." She yanked the bag from his hand. "I'll keep it." She crumpled the paper against her chest. "Maybe if I show him, he'll change."

Frowning, Lionel shook his head. "No guy changes because a woman is pregnant. He changes because he wants to change."

She shrugged. "Maybe he'll want to change for the baby."

She wasn't listening. He shook his head. He didn't want to argue. After years of working with teens and young adults, he always stated his case and walked away. Let them absorb the wisdom into their bones, either through trial and error or blind submission.

Beating sense into them didn't work. He strode across the room. As the pressure built in the back of his throat, he waved aside the plastic strip curtain and stepped into the front of the store. After flicking on the fluorescent lights, he gazed at the aisles lit like rows of opportunities, each one a different road to take, but none leading to where he wanted to go.

****

The one good thing Geraldine's father had taught her before he died was the importance of appearances. "Never let a customer know you're sad," he told her. "Always strive to hide your problems and focus on the solution. Your customers are always the solution." So when Geraldine arrived for her shift at eleven, she strode along the aisle with a sense of helpfulness. When a customer asked if they had any olives, Geraldine escorted the customer to the shelf and pointed out the different brands and varieties they carried—black and green, pitted or not pitted, whole or sliced. While working the register, she cupped each customer's hand, counting out the change and handing over the receipt. When the lunch rush started, she waltzed to the deli counter and whistled while she stacked lettuce and tomato and pickle on a roast beef sandwich.

The false good mood continued until she glanced over a customer's shoulder and witnessed Lionel touching Michelle's shoulder in the bread aisle. The tenderness of the gesture twisted her gut. Lowering the knife after cutting the sandwich in half, she leaned to the right, straining to see.

Michelle shifted out of view, leaving only Lionel hunched forward, talking.

Oh, how Geraldine wished she could hear what he

said.

The customer stepped back.

Annoyance bridled her shoulders. How dare the customer obliterate her sight? Bowing her head, she focused on wrapping the sandwich in white butcher paper. After writing the price with a black marker, she handed the package to the customer. With a tense smile, she waved. "Have a nice day."

By the time the customer strolled away, both Michelle and Lionel were nowhere to be seen.

A flash of panic seized her chest. With a tense smile, she acknowledged the next customer. "Someone will be right with you." She waved to attract Jeffrey's attention where he stood arranging heads of iceberg lettuce in the produce section. "Hey, sugar, can you take over?"

Nodding, Jeffrey finished with the lettuce and dismantled the cardboard box before striding toward the deli counter.

Could he walk any slower? With shaking fingers, she untied her apron and tossed it onto the counter. She glanced around the store, clicking her nails on the counter. Where could Michelle and Lionel have gone? She let her gaze linger on the plastic curtain leading to the employee break room, suddenly taken back to the moment she opened the door to the storeroom and caught her father with his pants around his ankles, his bare bottom exposed as he thrust into a younger employee bent over a shelf, her brown breasts swinging like pendulums as she tossed back her head and moaned. A cold shudder weakened her knees. She leaned against the sink, waiting for Jeffrey to arrive.

What would she say when she found Lionel and

Michelle alone? Would she be too shocked at what she discovered to open her mouth and say anything?

An ocean of time passed before Jeffrey nudged her aside to wash his hands and tie an apron around his waist.

"Thanks, sugar." Geraldine squeezed down the two steps and shimmied to the back of the store. Slashing aside the plastic curtain, she strode into the employee lounge.

Michelle stood, covering her face with her hands.

Lionel drew her into his arms and whispered something into her ear.

Glancing around, Geraldine wished she had something loud and obnoxious to garner their attention. Instead, she slapped her hand on the break room table. "What's going on?" The sharpness of her voice sliced the air.

Lionel sprung away from Michelle. A frown burrowed deep in his face. With one swift motion, he shoved a hand into a pocket and withdrew his wallet. After placing a twenty in Michelle's palm, he squeezed her hand closed. "Go across the street and get some lunch." He nodded. "Don't worry. I'm paying you for the time. I just need to talk to the missus."

Sniffing, Michelle cowered for a second before tucking the bill into her pocket and leaving through a back door.

The air lightened with the girl's absence. Geraldine crossed her arms over her chest and shifted her weight to one hip. "No more secrets. You either tell me exactly what is going on or I fire the girl."

He flushed bright red. A vein throbbed in his forehead. "I can't tell you anything. I made a promise.

You, of all people, know I keep my promises." When he spoke, he trembled. "And you can't fire her because I'll just hire her back."

Every molecule of her body tensed. How dare he be more concerned about the girl? She ground her teeth. "Your loyalty belongs to me and not her, understand?"

"No, the problem is *you* don't understand." Scowling, he pointed a thick finger toward her chest. "This situation has nothing to do with you. I will not tolerate your meddling. Leave us alone."

With a sharp intake of air, she squared her shoulders. "Are you having an affair?"

He threw up his arms and tossed back his head. "How can I possibly be having an affair when I can't even make love to my wife?" He dropped his arms and shook his head. "The Great Spirit told Michelle to come to me. She listened. If you want to know anything else, go talk to your witchy-woman friend and ask her to help you. Stop pestering me."

"But I'm your wife. I need to know." She clasped her hands together.

"No, you don't." He shoved a hand into his pocket and removed the keys to his truck. Without a word, he pivoted and strode toward the back door.

"Lionel, we aren't finished."

"I am." Lifting the keys overhead, he kept walking.

She placed her hands on her hips. How dare he avoid a confrontation? "Lionel James Jones, you can't leave."

He stopped and pivoted. "Don't talk to me like the kids we never had." His voice cracked. With his back to her, he stormed out the door.

"Lionel! Lionel!" For a long moment, she couldn't

decide whether to run after him or leave him alone. When the door slammed shut, the empty sound echoed throughout the high ceilings. She slumped into the nearest chair, folded her arms on the sticky table, and buried her head in the dark cavern. Oh, how could things between them go from bad to worse?

Chapter Seven

In his pickup truck, Lionel tore out of the parking lot. Dust kicked up around the squealing tires. What if he stopped at the diner and took Michelle with him? He grimaced. No, he didn't need any more complications than he already had. Turning onto the freeway, going north toward Eureka, he drove with the windows rolled down. Hot air spat into his face. The blazing afternoon sun pulsed against his skin.

He hadn't been this angry in years. Not since his parents died, leaving him nothing. The bulk of their estate went to his sister, a woman he hadn't spoken with since she left for New York after high school, never to return. The injustice of being neglected after a lifetime of dedication left a sour taste in his mouth and a jaded stride in his step. He was the one who sat in the hospital room, alerting the nurses for more water, another blanket, or a consultation with the doctor, while his sister broadcasted her smile on the evening news. Sure, he could understand his parents' motivation, their pride in their daughter's fame, but he couldn't comprehend the lack of common decency in not leaving anything to the son who stayed with them to the end.

Turning off the freeway, he drove east toward Wapi Mountain. Out of all of his friends, he hoped Nick might be home. He wanted to talk with someone who could commiserate over his situation, and no one knew about the irritations of women better than Nick who had dated too many women for too little time until he swore off them altogether. Shaking his head, Lionel wondered how that witchy woman, Hope, had shattered that promise.

He left the main road and swerved onto a private driveway that had been widened and paved when Nick's father asked for the sacred site in exchange for the land that now housed Vine Valley Casino. The scent of redwood trees floated into the cab, filling his senses with the calm rhythms of nature. Now that Nick had married Hope, Lionel wondered if the property would be left to the tribe after Nick died since he had no children. Just like Lionel. Both of them were childless with something of a legacy—Wapi Mountain for Nick, Larry's Deli for Lionel. Didn't matter if the deli was Geraldine's inheritance; his marriage to her and the time and money he invested in the store guaranteed him fifty percent, now and forever.

By the time he drove into the circular driveway at the top of the mountain and cut the engine, he no longer blazed with anger like a rushing river but pulsed with discontent like a trickling creek. He hopped out of the truck and arched his lower back. The stiffness reminded him of his age. Time was running low, as low as his patience with Geraldine.

Why couldn't he help a young pregnant woman who was still technically a teen without his wife running interference? Why did his wife always overshadow him, questioning his actions, demanding explanations for his motivations, and never quite leaving him alone? At first, when they were younger, her attentions seemed flattering. Now that they were older, her constant prying intruded on his privacy. Lionel climbed the stone steps and rang the doorbell.

The speaker beside the door crackled. "C'mon in, LJ, I'm just finishing with a client."

The lock on the door clicked.

Lionel rotated the knob, and the door opened. He had not been to Nick's place since Nick married Hope, and the change to the home surprised him. Instead of the full-length mirror beaming back his reflection the moment he stepped into the foyer, he glimpsed the pelt of a black bear hanging from the wall.

Hope's first husband, Richard, had been an avid hunter until cancer shot him down. The Wapi Museum housed the majority of the Richard Spencer collection. Lionel guessed Hope must have kept some of her favorite trophies to soften the otherwise sterile environment.

Laughter rumbled down the staircase. Nick escorted his client, a tall redheaded man in a suit, to the front door.

"Elliot, this is Lionel Jones, the co-owner of Larry's Deli and captain of the Vine Valley Crushers." Winking, Nick jabbed Lionel's shoulder. "And this is Elliot Flynn, the new owner of Jasper's Bar and Grill." He waved toward the man in the suit.

As he shook Elliot's hand, Lionel studied the stranger. He recognized the charm glittering in the man's green eyes. He had met many businessmen like Elliot during his life—flirtatious with the women while maintaining an aloof and unattainable mystique, disarming in business negotiations that benefited him more than the other party while maintaining a position of lovable innocence. Elliot was the type of man Lionel liked to refer to as an opportunist. He preferred to keep his distance. "Pleased to meet you."

"Likewise." Elliot squeezed his hand. "Friends call me Old Red."

"Okay, Old Red." Lionel wasn't about to offer his nickname of LJ to a guy he had just met.

After shaking Lionel's hand, Elliot turned and left.

Nick loosened the blue tie around his neck and pointed toward the backyard. "I'll meet you outside. I'm going to change, and we can toss the ball while we talk."

Lionel strolled through Nick's home. Woven tribal rugs covered the hardwood floor, and Wapi pottery graced the shelves in the kitchen. The objects mingled well with Richard's landscape paintings hanging in the living and dining rooms. Lionel remembered attending the grand opening of Richard's gallery years ago. A pang seized his chest. Hope almost lost the gallery to foreclosure until Geraldine suggested Nick help Hope with a refinance. Coming here without his wife knowing smelled almost like betrayal. Why had he promised Michelle not to tell anyone? Even he didn't understand his reasoning.

He opened the French doors leading to the deck. Heat patted his face. Below the deck, a space had been cleared in the grass to mimic a softball field. All around him, the panoramic view of the valley spread, east from the Wapi River cutting through the redwood forest to the streets and buildings of downtown, west to the vineyards and rugged Northern California coastline. The mountain was high enough to avoid morning fog, but low enough to retain a comfortable level of oxygen.

Nick strolled onto the deck and clapped a hand on

Lionel's shoulder. He placed a glove into his hand and waved toward the field below. "If you want, I can set up the net for batting practice."

"No, I can't stay long." Lionel slipped on the glove and followed Nick to the freshly mown lawn. "I have to get back to the store."

"What brings you out here?" Nick launched a ball.

Lionel caught the ball in his glove and tossed it back. Tension snaked across his shoulders. "Geraldine and I had a fight about her minding her own business. She called me by my full name like I was a child."

Snickering, Nick shook his head. "Did you storm off in a rage?"

"Floored the accelerator in the truck and made it here in fewer than twenty minutes."

Nick widened his eyes. "You must have been really mad."

The weight of the ball in the palm of his hand soothed him. "I hate women problems. They're so hard to fix."

"What happened?"

Watching the ball arc through the air, Lionel focused on Michelle's pregnancy. "I have a secret, and I can't tell her. She'll gossip. Turn things ugly."

"You can't keep secrets from your wife." Nick held the ball. "That's worse than playing with fire."

Sighing, Lionel dipped his head. "I was hoping for advice, not admonishment."

"If Geraldine's like Hope, she'll find out sooner or later." Nick wound his arm for a pitch. "Ready?"

Lionel nodded, poised to catch.

"Come clean." Nick released the ball. "Avoid the drama."

Sunlight cut through the clouds and across his vision. Squinting, he missed the ball. A nagging worry twisted his gut. He never failed a catch.

"Hey, boys!"

The sonorous voice pierced the stillness of the summer air, and he swiveled to glimpse Hope standing tall as a redwood tree on the deck. She wore a caftan dress in earth tones that fell just above her bare feet. Her long, black hair swung loose over her shoulders. Bracelets jangled on her wrists.

"Hey, baby!" Nick darted up the stairs, scooped his wife into his arms, and twirled until she tipped back her head and giggled.

Squatting to pick up the ball, Lionel stared at the happy couple. The memory of last night's failed romantic interlude punched his gut. Standing, he tossed the ball into the glove. The knots in his shoulders unraveled. He should return to the store and tell Geraldine the truth. Maybe she could help Michelle better than he could. After all, she had been pregnant once. She would know what to do.

As soon as she landed on her feet, Hope strode to the edge of the deck, her brown hands cupping the railing. "Nicky says you need to talk to me. Would you like a cup of tea?"

"Sure." Lionel swallowed the tightness in his throat. He hoped Nick hadn't disclosed his marital problem. In the kitchen nook, he sat on the window seat and folded his hands on the table.

Hope boiled a kettle of water and poured the steaming liquid into two mugs. Smiling, she set the mugs on coasters on the table. "Milk or sugar?"

Shaking his head, he curled his fingers around the

warm mug. With the heat of summer, his first choice of beverages would have been a beer. But he didn't want to ask for something else. Hope relied on tea the way Geraldine relied on sandwiches—for bonding. He sniffed the aroma of ginger and turmeric and let the smells work their magic.

"Do you want a reading?" Hope sat on a chair and leaned forward.

The piercing expression in her dark eyes haunted him. He didn't want someone peering into his soul. He liked his privacy. Didn't anyone know that? Taking a sip, he let the pungent, earthy-sweet taste linger on his tongue before he spoke. "I have a friend who needs help. She lives on the reservation. I thought you might know if there are any services available."

Hope frowned. "What type of services?"

"Medical and social services." He bowed his head. "She's unwed and pregnant. She doesn't know if she wants to keep the baby or not. Her boyfriend isn't exactly supportive." He raised his head and gazed into her eyes. "I think he might even be abusive."

Nodding, Hope took a deep breath and closed her eyes. Exhaling, she dropped her shoulders and inhaled again. After the third breath, with her eyes still closed, she relaxed into what looked like a trance, similar to a hypnotist he once saw on TV.

Lionel gripped the mug, letting the heat seep into his skin and warming the rest of his body like a slight fever. Glancing around the room, he searched for an exit. Even if he slid out of the window seat, he would have to walk past Hope to leave. He didn't want to disturb her. Some part of him worried she might put a curse on him. He didn't understand the spiritual hocus-

48

pocus she practiced.

Finally, after a loud exhale, Hope opened her eyes.

The gravity in her solemn expression thumped against his chest. He released his grip on the mug, leaned back against the warm window panes, and folded his arms over his chest. If he could have plugged his ears with his fingers without appearing rude, he would have. He didn't want to hear whatever she had to say.

"The Great Spirit sent a message." She held his gaze. "Red."

"Red?" He released his arms from his chest and leaned forward. "Like the color?"

She nodded. "This problem you have will only bring red."

"What does that mean?" He hated when people spoke in riddles. Red meant anger. Of course, he was red with rage. Who wouldn't be upset over hiding a secret from his wife to protect a young woman who needed his help? "Is red a code word for something else?"

Her solid and reassuring presence wavered in disturbing silence. Finally, she touched his wrist.

Her fingers were ice.

"Leave her alone. Let her solve her own problems."

A flash of resistance tightened his jaw. What good was leaving the girl alone? Didn't Hope understand he couldn't do that?

"I know you mean well." She removed her fingers from his wrist. "Bring her to me, and I'll take her to the clinic. She'll be okay. I promise."

Exhaling, he stared at the table, blank as a sheet of

paper. He didn't know if he could surrender Michelle's care to someone else, even if he trusted Hope. Some part of him needed to be right beside her like a father, caring for her, even though she wasn't his daughter. She was little more than an employee who had reached out because she said the Great Spirit said he could be trusted. How could he break that trust by surrendering her care to someone else?

Scooting to the edge of the window seat, he stood. "The Great Spirit told this woman to come to me for help because I could be trusted." He spread his arms wide. "Now the Great Spirit tells me to leave her alone because her problems will only bring me trouble." He shook his head and dropped his arms to the sides. "I don't understand this hocus-pocus. Can't your god stop doing the merry-go-round and get the story straight the first time around?"

Hope straightened her lips. "Sometimes the Great Spirit leads us on a journey that follows a circuitous path."

Damn riddles. He huffed. Whatever happened to direct communication? Glancing out the window, he waved goodbye to Nick. Turning back to Hope, he gestured to the mug on the table. "Thanks for the tea and the advice from the Great Spirit, but I think I'll go alone on this one."

****

Arranging a display of tomatoes, Geraldine inspected a firm plump fruit between her fingers. Worry knotted in her chest. How did she and Lionel drift so far apart, especially in regards to business? She stacked the tomato on the growing pyramid and selected another. With her fingertips, she squeezed the soft squishy middle and set aside the fruit in the remainder bin to be donated to the homeless shelter. A smashed tomato oozing with mold sat at the bottom of the box, and she tossed aside that one for the compost pile. The plastic curtain fluttered, and she glanced up.

Michelle stepped into the produce section, strapping her apron around her waist. Without a word, she picked up the remainder bin and carried it to the back with the other slightly damaged, day old, and past prime groceries.

She appeared tired and broken, hardly a threat. So why did Geraldine feel the heat rise to the surface of her skin and her hands clench into fists?

Michelle returned for the compost bin, hugging the box close to her body.

Geraldine raised a hand. "Can I talk with you?"

Michelle cowered, ducking her head and lifting her shoulders, shielding her face with the box.

"Oh, sugar, don't be scared." Frowning, Geraldine lowered her hand. Was someone beating that girl at home? Was that why she was so skittish? Or did Geraldine just come across as a hostile and abusive boss? She took a step back. "I just want to help." She softened her voice.

Michelle peered over the box.

Her wide eyes smoldered with distrust.

The bell on the glass doors tinkled.

Lionel stepped into the store.

Michelle skittered away.

Alone, Geraldine glanced over at her husband. He lumbered toward her with that wild rage burning in his brown eyes, jaw tensed, and hands clenched at his sides. She held her breath, knowing this moment was not a good time to talk.

He stopped and pointed toward the plastic curtain. "Let's go upstairs to the office."

Tension braided up the backs of her legs. She released her breath and fluttered her eyelashes. She hoped against reason he wanted to pick up from last night, fall into her arms, and smother her with kisses. More likely, he wanted to lecture her. She straightened her apron and glanced around the store. Only a few customers lingered in the aisles. Not too many to overwhelm the employees. She followed him up the stairs and into the office with stale air as hot and thick as molasses. She sank into the desk chair and swiveled. The backs of her thighs stuck to the warm leather seat. She squeezed her lips together and waited.

He flicked on the switch. A ceiling fan whirred to life, spinning heat around the room. He shut the door and broadened his stance, crossing his arms over his chest. "I had every intention of coming here and telling you everything until I found you harassing the poor girl." He flung his arms wide. "How can I trust you to do the right thing when you can't even honor my request to leave her alone?"

She trembled. The only other times he displayed this level of anger were after his parents died leaving him nothing and after the Vine Valley Crushers lost the World Masters by one run. "I'm sorry, sugar. I only want to help."

Exhaling, he dropped his arms to the sides and knotted his hands into fists. "She doesn't want your help." He gulped and steadied his voice. "I do."

"You do?" she echoed, leaning forward. Didn't he want her to leave him alone, too? After standing, she rushed over, every muscle in her body softening. "How can I help?"

"I don't know. I have to figure that one out." He slumped against the wall and stared at his feet. "I'm the only one Michelle trusts. But I don't know how to assist her without breaking her trust." A muscle in his jaw twitched. "I wish we had been parents. Then I think I would know what to do."

The heartbreaking sadness in his voice ached in her chest. "Ah, sugar, we *do* know what to do. We parent our employees." She touched his shoulder. She didn't understand what parenthood had to do with Michelle's problem unless... "Is she pregnant?"

He jerked up his head. "Why do you think that?"

She shrugged, dropping her hand from his shoulder. "You mentioned parenting."

Closing his eyes, he sighed. "I just feel protective of her. Like she's my kid, and not my employee, you know?" Opening his eyes, he met her gaze. "And, yes, she is pregnant."

"Oh, my." She gasped, her hand fluttering to her mouth. "No wonder she's scared as a kitten. For a moment, I thought she was abused." Everything suddenly fell into place—the emotional hug on the surveillance camera, the tear-swollen eyes, and the reluctance to open up to another woman for fear of judgment or sympathy rather than acceptance and understanding.

"I think she is abused, but I have no proof." He rubbed his forehead and pinched the skin between his eyes. "She hasn't even told the father, that no-good boy who drops her off and picks her up each day. If he doesn't want the baby, she might not go through with the pregnancy." He groaned. "Either way, I'll need to get her to a doctor."

"Can Hope help?" She grabbed the office phone on the desk.

He touched her wrist. "I already spoke with her. She's offered to take Michelle to the clinic on the reservation."

"Problem solved." A wave of relief washed over her.

"Not really." He crossed his arms over his chest. "I don't want to give her to someone she doesn't know or trust. I want to be with her every step of the way, whatever she decides to do."

"Don't make her problems your problems." She glowered, and a line of tension snagged between them. "Michelle must have other adults in her life who can help with this decision. She doesn't need you."

Bowing, he shook his head from side to side. "She's all alone, except for the boyfriend. I have to do the right thing, GG, and that's to see this situation to the end." He lifted his face. "She came to me first. She trusts me. Don't you understand? I can't abandon her."

The desperation in his voice startled her. She took a step forward. "I'll take her to the doctor."

"No, she doesn't trust you." Turning, he stepped away. "It has to be me."

The fury in his eyes matched the fierceness in his voice. "Okay." As soon as she surrendered, she plunged into the distance between them, lost in a sudden abyss.

Chapter Eight

Lionel squatted behind the batter with his glove raised and squinted at the blazing sun in the late afternoon sky. Fine dust and sticky sweat clung to the inside of his softball cap. He tugged it lower and focused on Cassidy on the pitcher's mound. The Vine Valley Crushers had made it through the first two days of the Western National Senior Softball Tournament in Sacramento, California, only to lose the third game of the day. With the stakes raised to double elimination, the team had to win this game against the Carson City Diggers if they wanted a chance of winning the tournament. Otherwise, they would go home, having lost their opportunity to compete against the Eastern National Senior Softball champion for the title of World Masters in Las Vegas next month.

Cassidy threw a high, underhanded pitch.

The batter swung and hit the ball toward right field.

Nick jogged backward with his gloved arm raised and caught the fly ball.

Three outs.

"All right, Crushers! Let's bat!" Standing, Lionel strode to the dugout and took a swig of cold water from the camping canteen Geraldine refilled between games. The Vine Valley Crushers needed to score one run to tie the game, two or more to pull ahead, during this final inning. "We need to get as many runs as we can during this open inning or we go home."

Nick, Cassidy, and the other teammates dropped their gloves and grabbed their bats.

Glancing up into the bleachers, Lionel waved to Geraldine.

She ignored him, too busy talking with Elliot.

Irritation bristled up his spine. Lionel didn't understand why Nick invited him. At forty-eight, the guy was too young to play with the seniors. At first, sitting in the bleachers with the wives and girlfriends didn't seem like a consolation prize until he noticed the unsolicited attention Elliot received from the women.

Deb fawned on him, buying him sodas from the concession stand.

Hope doted on him, offering some of her homemade fry bread.

And Geraldine touched his wrist as she talked, her giggles drifting across the field like an unwelcomed breeze.

Lionel tipped the canteen into his mouth and gulped the last swallow.

Even Noelle, who sat at Geraldine's feet, nudged her nose against Elliot's hand, begging to be petted.

"You're up, boss." Cassidy jabbed his shoulder. "Swing low toward center. The shortstop can't catch."

Grunting, Lionel gripped his bat tighter and stepped out of the dugout. All season, he had struggled with his swing, unable to find the sweet spot that would cause the ball to sail out of the park like he had years ago, before the arthritis limited the movement of his spine. When he focused, he could still hit, not as far and not as fast, just enough to get by as an average player. But the team didn't need average today. Today, they needed a hero.

From the bleachers, the women cheered. "Go, Lionel, go!"

"Hit a home run, sugar!" Geraldine's voice rose higher than the others.

With the bases loaded and two outs, Lionel stood before the plate and stared at the pitcher. If he didn't get this hit, then both the game and the tournament were over. Inhaling, he raised his bat and lowered his knees into position, keeping his feet planted on the ground. He hadn't drunk too much with the guys last night, and he hadn't indulged in Geraldine's advances. He left the restaurant early and soaked in the hot tub before falling asleep. As soon as the sunlight poked through the thin curtains of the hotel room, he stretched his stiff joints, his mind still groggy, both sore and mentally fatigued from yesterday's five, mostly back-to-back games.

At this rate, the seasons he had left to play were numbered. Unless some miracle restored his body to peak performance, he might eke out another five years, not the twenty he had hoped. How he longed for the power and precision of his youth when he could hit several home runs each game. Back then, he was the best batter, even better than Nick.

Okay, focus. He exhaled, digging the soles of his shoes into the dirt and shifting his hips from side to side. From behind, Geraldine's voice floated like bubbles and Elliot's deep laughter popped each one. They were too friendly and too familiar for a pair of strangers who only met yesterday. He breathed in again, eyeing the pitcher, but images of Old Red pressing his shoulder against the arm of his Golden Goddess and her fingers brushing against the back of his hand burned like the sun in his eyes.

Oh, why couldn't he concentrate? Worry lodged into his joints. The old love he had for his wife could not compare to the thrill of attention from someone younger. The muscles of his neck and upper back tightened. Yes, he had a depth of love that spanned over thirty years of history, but what little did the past matter when greeted with someone new? He gripped the bat tighter. The ball arced, and he swung and missed.

"Strike." The umpire clenched a fist.

Exhaling, he hung his head low and shook out his shoulders.

"You've got this hit, sugar." Geraldine's voice lilted above the others who shouted and cheered.

Inhaling, he focused on the batter. Raising the bat toward his shoulder, he leaned over the plate, ready.

The pitcher lobbed the ball.

He swung and missed. Again. Humiliation prickled his face.

"Strike."

Damn it. He lowered the bat against the dirt and spat bitterness from his mouth. He wanted to glance behind him and acknowledge the support of the women in the bleachers, but he couldn't risk locking gazes with Old Red or glimpsing his wife's fingers on another man's wrist. With the back of his hand, he wiped the sweat from his forehead. Lifting the bat, he shifted into position. One last time...

The pitcher tossed the ball.

A soft, easy pitch propelled toward him. Any beginner could hit it.

He swung hard, pain ripping through his joints. The tip of the bat missed the edge of the ball.

"Out."

The Carson City Diggers threw their gloves and hooted and hollered with victory.

Hot shame splashed against Lionel. He dragged his body back into the dugout.

"Don't worry." One of the players tapped his shoulder.

"You did your best." Cassidy nudged his arm.

"The sun must have been in your eyes." Nick patted his back.

As he sank onto the bench, Lionel glanced toward the bleachers.

Geraldine tilted her head toward Elliot, who was talking.

Tension knotted his shoulders. What were they discussing? His strikeout? Or his inability to perform well in the bedroom? Despair left him cold, and he shuddered in spite of the ninety-degree heat. Swallowing the tightness in his throat, he lowered the cap over his stinging eyes. Defeat sagged against his shoulders. He lost the game. With a fist, he rubbed his eyes. Would he also lose his wife?

****

The team gathered around the back of the Jones' pickup truck to commiserate over their loss. Geraldine stood beneath the paltry shade of a parking lot tree, holding Noelle's leash in one hand and a can of beer in the other. She tipped back the cold brew into her thirsty mouth. Without the prospect of winning the World Masters, she doubted they would travel so far from home next month to play three days of games just for fun.

Elliot broke away from the team and joined her.

"Too bad your husband struck out."

She shrugged. "He's getting older. Just like the rest of us." She tugged her lips into a frown.

"Not you, pretty lady."

With a sidelong glance, she caught a mischievous glint in his emerald eyes. Warmth powered through her body, and she gripped the can tighter. "Don't flatter me. I'm older than you are."

"And prettier." He lifted his can of beer and winked.

Heat flamed her face, and she tugged on Noelle's leash. A burning desire swept through her. Searching through the crowd, she landed her gaze on the jeering teammates who teased Lionel about the strikeout. Pity doused the flames of passion, leaving a cold, hard guilt wedged at the base of her spine. How could she bask in the glow of Elliot's flattery when her husband smoldered with humiliation?

"Hey, man, thanks for the beer." Nick tapped Lionel's shoulder. "You should strikeout every game." He laughed before he cracked the lid and guzzled.

Glancing from the guys to her husband, she caught the despondent expression in his brown eyes. A tug of pity yanked between her breasts.

Elliot nudged her arm. "If you and your girlfriends want to come by this week, I'll serve you an extended happy hour." He lifted the can above his head. "The first round will be on me."

She smiled. His invitation ignited a spark of excitement. "Sure thing, sugar. The girls and I will be there." She always enjoyed trying a new restaurant with Deb and Hope, but the prospect of spending the evening with Elliot filled her with unexpected pleasure. She let her gaze slide away, remembering how his breath tickled her neck when he leaned close to whisper in her ear about his childhood adventures growing up in Ireland. Every nerve ending in her body tingled. After taking a sip of beer, she tugged on Noelle's leash. "C'mon, girl, let's find your daddy."

Lionel leaned against the tailgate, arms crossed over his chest, scowling.

Snuggling alongside him, she tucked Noelle beside his feet. "Let's tell the others we need to leave soon to get home before dark." She leaned over to peck his tense cheek, feeling Elliot's gaze. As soon as she swiveled, she stumbled across the endless green of his eyes. A wildfire blazed through her damped by a shower of guilt. Maybe happy hour at Jasper's Bar and Grill wasn't such a good idea.

Lionel tilted his head. "I have a better idea. Let's leave now. I'm tired of the teasing." He packed the leftovers and loaded Noelle into the backseat.

Geraldine found Hope and Deb loitering by Nick's RV. "We're getting ready to leave. Just came to say goodbye and invite you to happy hour at Jasper's this week."

"I'll be there." Deb hugged her tight. "I'll let you know how the lingerie idea works."

"Okay, sugar." Geraldine had suggested her friend slip into something more comfortable to get into the mood for her husband's advances.

"I wouldn't miss it for the world." Hope squeezed her. "Be well, dear."

"Oh, I will, sugar." Geraldine released her. "I look forward to seeing you both at five o'clock at Jasper's Bar and Grill this Thursday." Swiveling, she cupped her hands around her mouth. "Hey, guys." She paused, waiting for their attention. "I don't care about the score—you all played well." She blew kisses to the teammates, waving her arm high and smiling like she was standing on a float during a parade.

Lionel held open the passenger's door and grabbed Geraldine's elbow as she stepped into the cab.

He was still a gentleman, after all these years. Heat rushed to her face. Why was she thinking about how far she could flirt with another man without jeopardizing her marriage? She tugged the hot seat belt across her chest and gazed out the window. All of her adult life, she had toed the line between guilt and innocence, dodging more than a few close calls. She loved to flirt, touching hands and wrists, calling everyone "Sugar." But her flirtatious dalliances ended once a man asked for her phone number. She would dismiss him with a quick, I'm-happily-married, thank-you-very-much response.

Once, a particularly insistent suitor followed her home, and she drove into the parking lot of the police station and waited until he left her alone. Another time, she dodged a young man's kiss, turning her head just as his lips met her chin. She knotted her hands into her lap, wondering how far she would let Elliot go.

Lionel started the engine and rolled down the windows while the air conditioner kicked on. He gripped the steering wheel until his knuckles glowed as white as his hair. With his gaze focused squarely on the road, he didn't speak.

Geraldine leaned against the hot leather seat and closed her eyes for a moment, luxuriating in the memory of sitting shoulder to shoulder next to Elliot, talking about anything other than the game. She didn't even remember the final score, only aware the team had lost by a very slim margin from Lionel's strikeout. Opening her eyes, she leaned forward and studied her husband. "Sometimes I feel like we're losing each other."

"I'm right here." He steered onto the freeway and rolled up the windows. Snapping on the radio, he played a popular song about love gone wrong. "I'm not going anywhere. Are you?" He flashed a glance before returning his attention to the road.

Swallowing the dryness in her throat, she dropped her gaze to her long manicured nails. How many seasons had it been since she kept the nails short and unpolished so she could run after the home-run balls and carry them back to the dugout for a congratulatory kiss from the captain of the team? One or two? She sighed, knowing the lapse had been longer. "Your mind is elsewhere."

"No shit." He slapped the steering wheel with the flat of his hand. "I'm disappointed in myself. I let down everyone. I not only lost the game, but the season." He shook his head. "That goddamn bystander you were so chummy with in the stands said I should sign up for the free batting clinic to improve my swing." He flashed a glance in her direction. "Some new friend you've got. Thinking I can't hit for shit."

"You can't." The words slipped out of her mouth before she could stop them. "I mean you were preoccupied. You've been that way since Michelle confided in you."

"Don't talk about Michelle. I wasn't thinking about her or her problems on the field." He sighed. "I was thinking of you."

"Me?" A zing of surprise zipped through her. She touched her chest with her cool fingertips to still her fluttering heartbeat.

Noelle wiggled her head above the seat and nudged her nose against Lionel's shoulder.

He patted her with one hand, steering the truck with the other. "Good girl, Noelle. Did you have a great time watching your papa play?"

"Of course, she did, sugar." Relief at the momentary distraction soothed the terror building in her chest. "She doesn't care whether you win or lose."

"Do you?" He snuck a glance in her direction.

"I just want you to have fun." She lowered her voice to a gentle hum, hoping her words would heal his crushed soul. But a dizzying fear spiraled into her mind. "Why were you thinking of me when you should have been focused on the ball?"

He flicked on the indicator, glanced over his right shoulder, and steered into the middle lane to let a car pass. "We haven't exactly been the best lovers for each other the past year. Seeing you flirting with Old Red reminded me of that fact."

"Old Red?" She arched an eyebrow.

"Elliot."

The name fell flat from his lips, but the vibrations sent ripples throughout her. She curled her toes in her sandals, chanting the different labels in her mind: Elliot, Old Red, new owner of Jasper's Bar and Grill. She bit her lower lip, thinking of a potential one to add to the list—lover boy. "Don't worry about Elliot." She shifted against the seat, peeling the backs of her thighs from the leather. "He's harmless."

"He's a womanizer. I don't want him preying on my Golden Goddess."

The old familiar nickname flickered in her mind. She remembered the first time he whispered those words after he kissed her beside the apple tree in her parents' front yard. "You're my Golden Goddess. I worship you." She trembled. Did he still worship her?

Noelle sat back, leaving them alone.

Lionel held Geraldine's hand, curling his calloused fingers over her palm.

Staring at the passing cars, she swallowed a lump of nervousness. A knot tightened in her stomach. "Elliot invited us girls to happy hour this week. Do you mind if we go?" She flicked a sidelong glance, seeking permission.

"I'd rather you go someplace else, but I trust you." He squeezed her fingers.

With her other hand, she patted the back of his hand. "I'll be with the girls. I'm not going alone." She wanted to reassure him, but more importantly, she wanted to convince herself she could be trusted to toe a line of desire without tipping into a pool of lust.

Chapter Nine

Lionel stooped to count the number of boxes delivered in the early morning fog. Down the street, the engine of a hot rod growled. He stood, arching his back and narrowing his gaze.

Moments later, a flashy, red sports car whipped into the parking lot, its wheels turning donuts twice before screeching to a stop. The passenger door flicked open, and Michelle stepped out, her long hair covering her face as she leaned over to say goodbye to the driver. As soon as she closed the door, she stepped back. The sports car bolted out of the parking lot and up the street.

The stench of rubber burned Lionel's nostrils. He hated the damn, irresponsible boyfriend who acted like he was thirteen and not thirty. He had met the guy only twice—once when Michelle interviewed for the job and again when she attended the annual company picnic earlier in the summer.

Paul "Firewalker" Hughes was a tall, lanky man with tattoos littering his arms and long hair braided between his shoulders. He always smelled of weed and booze covered up by cheap cologne. When Lionel asked Michelle what she saw in the guy, she bowed her head and whispered he was "good in bed."

Anger clenched his fists. Why did sex elevate a boy to a man in a young woman's eyes? He glanced at the opened box at his feet and slumped. Hell, even his wife would say she needed a man who was "good in bed," and she wasn't a young woman anymore. Shame and embarrassment splashed his face. Oh, when exactly had he stopped being that man who was good in bed? He couldn't remember any more.

"Hello." Michelle brushed past him and headed toward the employee lockers to stow her purse. She knotted her hair into a pony tail, tied the company-issued apron around her waist, and tugged the long sleeves over her forearms.

Over a week had passed since the pregnancy test, and Lionel could not convince her to see a doctor, either on or off the reservation. "You have health insurance as one of your employee benefits," he had said the day after the test results. "Use it." But she had one excuse after another—from the fact the boyfriend shadowed her any time she wasn't at work to the fear of making a decision. "If you wait long enough, nature will decide for you," Lionel had said yesterday.

"We're lucky we aren't on a residential block or that boyfriend of yours would wake the whole neighborhood by the way he drives." Lionel grabbed the steel hand truck to wheel one of the boxes into the store to replenish the canned goods section.

Michelle followed him into the empty store. "I'll restock the shelves."

He parked the box in the middle of an aisle and placed a fist against his hip. "You make a decision yet?" The anxiety of not knowing left him unable to help, which escalated the uneasiness stirring deep in his gut whenever he was around her.

Bowing her head, she sighed. "I haven't told Paul yet."

"Why not?" He stepped away from the hand truck and dropped his arms to the sides.

Biting her lower lip, she shook her head. "I don't want him to get angry and blame me."

"Honey, it takes two to tango." The cliché rolled off his tongue. "If he doesn't want the consequences, then he shouldn't play."

She tugged on her shirt sleeves.

Narrowing his gaze, he studied the nervous gesture. Oh, why didn't he just give up trying to help her and admit defeat? She didn't need him any way. She was a grown woman with a grown-up decision to make. Let her make it on her own.

But he couldn't.

"Why don't we make an appointment to see a doctor during work hours? I'll stay in the waiting room until the appointment is over." He paused, searching his thoughts for any objections he might encounter. "Don't worry about the hours. I'll pay you for them as part of your sick time, okay?"

She rubbed her arms with her hands. "Why are you so kind to me?"

Something softened inside of him, and he relaxed his stance. He wanted to pull her into his arms and protect her from every bad thing in the world. "My wife was pregnant with twins about twenty years ago. We lost them. My daughter would have been around your age. When I see you, I think of her."

A tentative smile blossomed.

"You would have been a great father." She stepped forward and embraced him. "I'm so glad the Great Spirit sent me to you."

Safe in a spot without surveillance cameras or

other employees, he held her close, cupping her upper back with his hands, feeling the warmth of security and peace flood through him. He didn't care about his wife discovering the inappropriate dynamic growing between him and Michelle. He only cared about being a father-figure. Squeezing his eyes shut, he imagined the woman in his arms as his daughter, his flesh and blood, not his employee. "I love you, Michelle, and I want you to make the right decision for you and your baby, no matter what obstacles you have to overcome." He released her then grasped her by the shoulders. "I'm here for you. If you want even more support, I can ask my wife and her friends for assistance. They're women. Some of them have been pregnant. They've all been young. They might be better equipped to help you than I am."

She nodded. "I'll think about it."

"Don't think too long."

Without a word, she stepped away to open the box and restock the shelves.

After a moment, Lionel shrugged a shoulder and steered the hand truck toward the storeroom. The metal clanged and rattled next to his shuffling feet. Through the open loading dock, a cool breath of morning air exhaled against his freshly shaven face. In a matter of hours, the fog would lift and disperse, leaving the day sunny and exposed, showering the valley with buckets of heat. He stood on the landing, inhaling the moist air, calming the growing need he had to be a father to a woman who was debating whether or not she wanted to be a mother to a child she hadn't planned.

Oh, why was life so unfair? He balled his hands into fists. Why did he miss the opportunity to parent when he wanted that experience more than he wanted anything in the world while others rejected the gift of parenthood as an unwelcome lifelong chore?

****

Geraldine stood before the mirror above the sink in the master bathroom of her house, fluffing her golden locks with her fingers. She debated about how much makeup she should brush across her face before meeting Deb and Hope at Jasper's tonight. She had left the store early, reminding Lionel of her girls' night out, and showered and changed into a new outfit for the excursion. The curve-hugging, low-cut blouse and form-fitting jeans emphasized her good figure, but the bags under her eyes and the lines on her neck exposed her age. She glanced at the row of creams and cosmetics lining the shelf in the medicine cabinet and sighed. Even with a full face of makeup, she could not disguise what she wanted to deny—she wasn't a ripe plum promising tender skin and sweet juices; she was a withered prune.

After dusting her face and neck with powder and swiping eye shadow over her lids and mascara over her lashes, she swiveled a tube of coral lipstick and swept it across her lips. Blotting her lips with a square of tissue, she wondered if Elliot would notice the extra effort she put into her appearance tonight.

Fifteen minutes later, she yanked back the door of Jasper's Bar and Grill and stepped into the dark, wood-paneled room. The scent of sizzling steaks filled the warm air. On the left, a bank of booths lined one wall. On the right, a row of stools faced the mirrored bar. She glimpsed Hope and Deb sitting shoulder to shoulder at the bar, but she focused on Elliot who winked as he wiped a glass dry.

"Hey, pretty lady." Elliot smiled. "What's your poison?"

Geraldine glanced at Hope's whiskey and Deb's glass of red wine. "Cosmopolitan, please."

"Sophisticated, aren't we?" Elliot deepened his smile.

"Damn right, sugar." Geraldine winked, feeling heat rush to her cheeks. She was glad she had not worn any blusher.

Deb waved and Hope smiled.

Geraldine took a seat next to Hope.

"Good to see you." Hope swung her long black hair over one shoulder. "How's Lionel?"

Geraldine hung her purse strap on the hook beneath the bar. "Fine, I guess." Raising her eyebrows, she folded her arms on the counter. "He's not grumpy anymore about the loss, if that's what you mean."

Hope frowned, the skin between her eyebrows pinched. "He hasn't told you."

"About?" Tension snaked across Geraldine's shoulders. Why would Lionel confide in Hope about anything? Outside of softball and Nick, the two never crossed paths.

Tipping back the shot glass, Hope swallowed. She smacked her lips and set the empty glass on the bar.

"Another?" Elliot set down Geraldine's cosmopolitan and pointed to Hope's empty shot glass.

Nodding, Hope swiveled toward Geraldine, her caftan grazing Geraldine's legs. "I guess I shouldn't say anything if he hasn't told you."

Curiosity blossomed. "Tell me, sugar."

After a deep breath, Hope sighed. "He came by the

house a week or two ago. He and Nick were playing catch in the backyard. Nick said Lionel needed a consultation. We sat in the kitchen, and I spoke with the Great Spirit about a pregnant girl who lives on the reservation who Lionel wanted to help." She flashed a smile at Elliot to acknowledge the new drink before she grabbed Geraldine's hand. "I told him to bring her to me. He hasn't. I thought he might have gone to you."

Geraldine tugged away her hand. "Ah, sugar, he told me about the girl's problems, but he hasn't asked me to solve them for her." She sipped the cold, sweet liquor that warmed her insides. "He asked me to leave him alone. He wanted to fix it himself this time."

Deb leaned over the counter, her dark eyes wide, and her pixie cut highlighting her cheekbones. "I told Hope not to worry. Lionel isn't like Cassidy. He doesn't have a temper problem. He's as patient as a saint."

Elliot sidled up to them. "And does *this* saint want a refill?" He winked at Deb.

Bowing her head, Deb twirled the stem of the empty wine glass, her cheeks flushed.

Geraldine lifted her eyebrows and tugged her lips together in a straight line. A cold hard truth plunged into her stomach. Elliot flirted with every woman. Why did she think she was special?

Lifting her head, Deb nodded and slid the glass across the counter. "Yes, I'll have another." As soon as Elliot left, Deb swiveled toward Hope and Geraldine. "I took your advice, but I couldn't wear one of those tight, scratchy outfits any longer than a minute." She shuddered. "I'm hoping if I have one more drink I'll get relaxed, not too relaxed so I can't drive, just loose enough to respond to Cassidy's advances when I get home."

"At least someone's getting lucky tonight." The strain of jealousy thinned Geraldine's voice, and she took another sip of her drink to calm the swirling emotions lodged in her chest.

Elliot set down the fresh glass of wine.

Smiling, Deb nodded her thanks. She waited until he left to serve patrons at the other end of the bar before she spun toward Hope and Geraldine. "I hate feeling guilty when I turn him down." She took a sip of wine.

"That's your Catholic upbringing." Geraldine touched the glass to her lips and finished her drink. If there was a God, he had a sick sense of humor. Why pair the former nun with the horniest guy on the softball team?

Hope rubbed Deb's forearm. "A good relationship is not based on sex." The bracelets on her wrists jangled. "Nick and I have a strong connection. We share the same values and respect each other's differences."

After swallowing another mouthful of wine, Deb bowed her head. "I'm afraid I'll lose him because I really don't like sex." She sighed. "I like the intimacy afterward."

The tears in Deb's voice tugged at Geraldine. The jealousy melted away. "Ah, sugar, if he loves you, he'll never leave." Did Cassidy ever struggle with lustful stirrings of temptation whenever Deb avoided his attempts at lovemaking?

Hope shook her head. "I guess I'm the only one without any problems."

Geraldine covered her lips with a napkin to

suppress a snicker. Why would Hope have problems? She was married to the richest man in Vine Valley with the legacy of her first husband—God rest his soul—preserved for all eternity in the Wapi Museum. She lived on the sacred mountain and communicated with the Great Spirit. Best of all, she didn't have a gray hair or a wrinkle. Yes, genetics might have contributed to her youthful appearance, but who cared? A flush of anger rushed through Geraldine when she dwelled on the injustice of her friend's luck and her own damn misery. She didn't mind being working class and marrying for love, but she did mind the gray hairs and the crappy sex life.

Elliot brushed his fingers against Geraldine's wrist. "Hey, pretty lady, you ready for a second drink?"

A pulse jumped in Geraldine's hand, triggering an acceleration of her heartbeat. She stared at her empty martini glass. Could she handle another? She glanced up and met Elliot's intent gaze. Every cell in her body exploded with desire. Oh, why did she feel so young and alive in his presence? Swallowing, she nodded.

Elliot whisked away the glass, smiling.

Studying him as he worked, Geraldine absorbed every detail. How the overhead lights caught the strands of gold in his fiery hair. How the ropey muscles in his forearms bulged as he shook the cocktail shaker. How fine lines crinkled around his green eyes when he smiled. How his moist fingers cooled the back of her hand when their knuckles brushed as he placed the glass on the counter. "There you go, my pretty lady." He winked.

Heat rushed through Geraldine's body, and she dipped her head, hoping her friends did not notice her flaming cheeks.

Hope tossed a ten dollar bill on the counter and stood. "I'd love to stay longer, but I'm meeting Nick for a charity event tonight." She kissed Deb's cheek first then Geraldine's. "Enjoy dinner. See you both next week."

As soon as she left, Geraldine stole the seat next to Deb. She grabbed her reading glasses from the purse hanging against her knees and read the laminated menu. "Do you know what you're having?"

Deb sighed. "I really should go home and try to seduce my husband."

"If you're seducing anyone, you need some energy." Geraldine glanced at the heavy meat-and-potato dishes and winced, wondering if she should also pass.

Fishing in her purse, Deb removed a ten dollar bill and set it next to her empty glass of wine. "I feel like sex is penance for leaving God for a man." Tears glistened in her brown eyes, and she sniffled. "Sometimes I regret my decision. Cassidy is hard to live with, and his son requires constant care. I miss the days of being alone with my prayers, working in the garden, or kneeling before the altar. I miss that unconditional, uncomplicated love God had for me and me for him." She squeezed a napkin in her fist and dabbed the corners of her eyes. "I hate the fights and the making up afterward. I hate the constant battle of wills."

She stopped and stared at the counter. Her lips twitched into a smile. "But I do love those moments when everything feels just right—when Cassidy pitches a perfect game or when Adam says a few words or when I wake in the middle of the night, feeling scared and alone, and Cassidy drapes his arm over my shoulder and holds me close until I feel so warm and safe I drift back to sleep."

Geraldine took a sip of her sweet drink and nodded. "Love is a roller coaster except with more twists and turns." She'd spent more than half her life with Lionel. How could her future not include him? "I guess we're both lucky."

Elliot returned. "The luck of the Irish is better." He pointed to the menu in Geraldine's hands. "Have you decided?"

After glancing at Deb's bowed head and the ten dollar bill on the counter, Geraldine shook her head. "Looks like an early night."

"Too bad." He folded his arms and leaned closer. "I was hoping you'd stay 'til closing time."

If Geraldine bent at the waist, she could brush her lips against his lips and part his mouth with her tongue. The image propelled a rush of blood to her face. He was just inches away, and the scent of his musky cologne powered through her body, leaving her damp with desire.

What did he have in mind for the wee hours of the night? She tingled from her scalp to her toes. Oh, what he would feel like inside of her? Glancing away, she grabbed her purse. With trembling fingers, she placed a twenty dollar bill on the counter to pay for the two drinks and leave a generous tip. "Next time." She flashed a smile that sealed the promise.

"You can't pay more than your friends." He slid back the bill.

"That's all I have, sugar."

"Well, then." He folded the twenty in one hand and placed Deb's ten beside Geraldine's empty glass. "We're even."

Deb stood on wobbly knees. "Oops. I think I might have had too much."

Glancing at her watch, Geraldine registered the time as six thirty. "It's early. We'll walk it off."

"But then I'll be sober."

Geraldine stood and slipped her purse over her shoulder. "Better sober and sad than dead and mad."

Deb snickered.

The old drinking-and-driving joke from high school still held weight. Geraldine linked her arm with Deb's.

Elliot laughed. "The sober saint and the mad husband."

Lifting her brow, Geraldine tugged Deb closer. Elliot was a newcomer to Vine Valley. He didn't share the group's lifelong history. "Sugar, her husband would only be mad if she was dead."

Leaning against the counter, Elliot winked. "I'd be mad if she was sober."

So, he liked his women drunk. Geraldine widened her smile. "Night, Elliot."

He stood and waved. "Night to my sober saint." He held Geraldine's gaze a moment longer. "And my pretty lady."

A flicker of lust fanned deep in Geraldine's lower belly. Oh, how she wanted more than anything for that statement to be true. After stepping outside into the cooling air of an aleady long evening, she guided Deb along the sidewalk. Over the tops of the buildings, the breath of fog exhaled. With each step, she slumped beneath the weight of reality. She wasn't anyone's pretty lady. She was Lionel's wife, an aging golden goddess, walking arm in arm along the boulevard with her high school friend who could not manufacture desire for her new husband. She heaved a sigh. Oh, what an odd couple she and Deb made.

Chapter Ten

Lionel sat in the waiting room, flipping through a magazine, but he could not focus. After tossing the glossy pages onto the coffee table, he leaned forward with his hands clasped between his knees, gazing at the others in the medical clinic on a Friday afternoon.

A few pregnant women sat in the vinyl chairs, some with partners beside them, others alone. They either chatted with their partners or scrolled through their phones.

He unclasped his hands and rubbed his sweaty palms against his jeans. Above him, an air-conditioning vent blew cold air against his coarse skin. Soft instrumental music piped through the speakers at each corner of the room like a hypnotic lullaby. But he could not relax. He kept glancing at the door beside the reception desk, hoping Michelle would emerge with news which would help her make a decision.

When the nurse had asked if he wanted to come back with Michelle into the examination room, he had to bite the inside of his mouth not to respond. Of course, he wanted to be beside her, to listen to the doctor's report firsthand, but he was just an outsider, a concerned employer, and a caring friend. He was not the baby's father or a member of the family.

Sighing, he wished he could have stayed in his truck or returned to the store. But heat blazed like a furnace, and he didn't want Michelle to text him when she was ready to go back to work. He wanted to be here as soon as she stepped out of the examination room. He wanted to embrace her, ask her how it went, and reassure her everything would be all right. He also wanted no one to recognize him as he waited. The last thing he needed was a complication. Someone reporting back to his wife about his presence in the OB/GYN department of the medical facility would only spark rumors that would spread like wildfire.

"Mr. Jones?" The receptionist waved. "The doctor asked for you to come back to the examination room."

Touching his hand to his chest, he lifted his head and raised his eyebrows. "Me?"

The receptionist tilted her head to one side. "You are Mr. Jones, aren't you?"

Nodding, he stood. A swoosh of nausea rolled through his stomach, almost buckling his knees. Why would the doctor want to see him in the examination room? He hobbled across the waiting area, dodging the curious glances of the expectant women and their partners, and met a nurse at the door.

"Right this way." She pointed down a hall, blinding with its white walls and white linoleum, a back alley toward heaven.

He followed the maze, past closed doors with paper charts, around another nurses' station, past a standing scale and a private bathroom to another closed door.

The nurse knocked once before entering.

Michelle perched like a raven on the blue branch of the examination table. She lifted her shoulders, and her long black hair ruffled like feathers, as if she might launch off into flight.

The doctor stood on the opposite side of the narrow room. With his gaze focused on the monitor, he typed on a keyboard. "Your niece wanted you to come back and hear the news in person in case you had any questions."

His niece? The phrase shot through him. She had told the doctor they were kin. The muscles in his face softened. Taking a seat in the brown chair between the examination table and the computer, he held his breath, ready to hear whatever the doctor had to say.

Michelle touched his shoulder with her warm brown hand.

Without a word, he closed his fingers over hers.

As soon as he finished typing, the doctor nudged his glasses up the bridge of his nose and smiled. "The test results are positive for pregnancy. We did an ultrasound to see how far along. Ten weeks."

Michelle squeezed his fingers. "I got to listen to the heartbeat."

Turning, Lionel dropped her hand and searched her face. "Did you see the baby, too?"

As she shook her head from side to side, her long hair rustled against the paper gown. "The doctor said it's too early."

"No need for a sonogram yet." The doctor tapped his chest. "The fetus sounds healthy."

Ten weeks along with a heartbeat. Lionel bowed his head. A swirl of excitement and dread swooshed inside him. When he met Michelle's gaze, he could feel the vibration of her energy, a combination of hope and fear. "Have you made a decision?"

Swallowing, she studied her hands before lifting her face toward the doctor. "What are my options?"

Crossing his arms over his chest, the doctor leaned against the computer stand. "If you want to have the baby, you need to take a daily multivitamin and schedule a follow-up appointment for one month. If you want an abortion, you need to act within the next two weeks."

Lionel swiveled from the doctor's stoic face to Michelle's pinched one. Fourteen days. The taste of bile filled his mouth.

"I'll let you know soon." Michelle knotted her hands into her lap. "Thank you."

"My pleasure." He handed Lionel a card. "Call if you have any questions or if you want to schedule a follow-up appointment or an abortion." He strode toward the door. "Good luck."

After he left, Lionel stood and pointed with the business card. "I'll be in the waiting room."

She touched his arm. "Don't go."

"But you need your privacy to dress." He waved toward her paper gown.

"Turn around. I'll be quick." She slipped off the table and gathered her clothes.

With his back toward her, he stood, gazing at the blank wall. His jagged breath and the crinkle of her paper gown filled the tiny room. He bunched his hands at his sides and closed his eyes. Two weeks. By the first week of September, he would know whether he would need to hire a temporary worker during Michelle's maternity leave or give her two weeks off to mourn. Gulping a mouthful of air, he choked. How could anyone grieve any loss in a matter of days? Even now, some twenty years later, the tug of loss ached all out of proportion. The twins he never held were a constant absence in his arms. Oh, how could she not choose life?

"You can turn around."

Pivoting, he glanced at her slender body dressed in T-shirt and jeans. No baby bump showed.

She draped her work apron over the crook of one arm, her purse in the other. "Ready?"

How could anyone prepare for this type of decision? No matter how many pro and con lists were tallied, the results were the same. Live or die. Keep or lose. Each road a deliverance from the other with unanswered questions left along the way. He just didn't want her to carry the same regrets he did for things out of his control because she didn't need to be in his position. She held power over her body and her pregnancy. Win, lose, or draw, the choice was hers.

Leaving the heavy air of the examination room, he strode silently by her side down the maze of white corridors. The shuffle of his feet echoed like the pitter-patter of tiny heartbeats against the bare walls.

****

That night, Geraldine set the table for two. With oven mitts, she gripped the edges of the casserole dish and set it on a trivet in the center of the table. Steam wafted up, carrying the scent of basil, garlic, and rosemary. The last romantic meal failed. Surely, the outcome would be different tonight.

Lionel lumbered into the room, freshly showered and changed, with Noelle limping beside him.

After smiling, Geraldine pecked his lips.

He brushed his fingers through her hair and cupped the back of her neck, pressing his mouth firmly against hers.

A wind of desire swept through her, and she

dropped the oven mitts from her hands and wove her arms around his back, pressing the length of her body against him.

Noelle barked and nudged her wet snout between their legs.

Pulling away, Lionel chuckled and stroked the dog's head. "Okay, ol' girl. We'll get to the main course. But I won't promise you any scraps."

As soon as the firm warmth of Lionel's body left hers, Geraldine closed up, surrounded by an invisible wall of coldness. Bending, she picked up the oven mitts and disappeared into the kitchen. From the quartz counter, her cell phone pinged. She dropped the oven mitts on the counter and grabbed the phone, swiping to read the message from Deb.

—*Will you meet me at Jasper's next Thursday at eight for one drink? I want to get in the mood without getting drunk and falling asleep.*—

Glancing out the window overlooking the yard, Geraldine inhaled deeply. Delicate lavenders and pinks painted the evening sky. She believed walking for an hour would be enough to take the edge off the buzz Deb felt from drinking one too many glasses of wine. She didn't expect her friend to fall asleep as soon as she arrived home. After picking up her phone, she typed her response.

—*No problem, sugar. I'll pick you up. One drink, then straight home.*—

"Is everything all right?" Lionel stepped into the kitchen.

"It's just Deb having domestic problems." Geraldine placed her phone on the counter.

"Oh, no, here comes the gossip." Lionel chuckled,

wrapping his arms around her waist and nuzzling his nose against her neck. "At least, we don't have domestic problems."

She stiffened, wedging a hand against his chest. "What do you mean, we don't have problems?"

"Don't kill the mood, GG. I'm feeling fine tonight."

But for how long? She bit the inside of her mouth to prevent the thought from being spoken aloud. She didn't want any false hope. She only wanted release.

"Let's eat." He grabbed her hand and led her to the table.

She remembered the feel of Elliot's fingers against the back of her wrist, the wild meadows of his green eyes, and the hunger tugging deep in her belly. Sitting with Noelle curled beside her feet, she poured two glasses of wine and offered a toast. "To us."

Lionel clicked his glass against hers and smiled. "Tell me. How was your day?"

She laughed. "You were there."

Bowing his head, he cut into the casserole. "I left early to take Michelle to the doctor."

She had not noticed his absence. Raising her eyebrows, she studied his thick hands gripping the fork and knife. "How did the appointment go?"

"Fine." He chewed a mouthful of pasta and mozzarella and washed it down with a gulp of wine. "She's ten weeks pregnant. She got to listen to the heartbeat. The doctor said the baby sounds healthy." He dropped his gaze, and a muscle in his jaw twitched.

"Is she having the baby?" Geraldine swirled the wine in her glass. She imagined a baby shower—fun— and a search for a temporary employee to hire and train for the six-month maternity leave—not fun. She took a sip of the full-bodied cabernet sauvignon.

With the tines of his fork, he drew tracks through the tomato sauce. "She has two weeks to decide."

Two weeks. She dabbed her mouth with a napkin. "That's not a whole lot of time, sugar."

"I know." He met her gaze.

He appeared old and haggard. Concern creased new wrinkles on his forehead. No wonder he wriggled in the middle of night, tugging at the sheets, unable to sleep. No wonder he couldn't sustain the passion. He spent all of his energy focused on Michelle and her problems. Bitterness swept through her. She emptied her glass and poured another. No chance of getting lucky tonight.

The tension between them wove tighter throughout the rest of the meal. Only the clicks of their silverware and the occasional nudge from the dog punctuated the blanket of misery that had descended upon them.

After the leftovers had been stored and the dishes washed, Lionel wrapped his arms around Geraldine's waist. "Let's make love," he whispered.

The heat of his breath against her ear left her cold. How could she feign passion when all of his devotion rested with an employee who was young enough to be his daughter? She wrestled out of his embrace. "Not tonight."

He dropped his arms and broadened his stance. "Why are you turning me away when you complain you don't get enough sex?"

Tucking her arms under her breasts, she lifted her chin. "How can I get in the mood knowing you're thinking of her?"

"Her?" He wrinkled his forehead.

"Michelle." She pouted.

Tossing back his head, he scowled. "What does she have to do with us?"

She swallowed, forcing her lips into a straight line. "She's all you think about." A prickle of guilt inched across her scalp. Like Elliot was all she thought about. She was as much to blame as Lionel. But she shoved aside the recognition and projected her frustrations onto their pregnant employee, as if that act alone could extinguish her desire for Elliot.

"That's not true." He stepped forward and grasped her hands. "Right now, I'm thinking I want to strip you out of that dress and kiss you all over."

Sniffing, she let him take her cool hands in his warm ones. Why was he so obsessed over Michelle's pregnancy? Tears clogged her throat and burned her eyes. "Are you still upset we never had kids?"

He tugged her close and squeezed her hands. "Upset is the wrong word." He rubbed his mouth against her hair. "Disappointed is a better word. Lost is probably the best word."

Pressure squeezed her chest. "You feel lost because we didn't have kids?" She phrased the statement like a question, her voice lifting at the end.

He brushed his lips against her cheek, his mouth pausing by her ear. "She told the doctor I was her uncle because she wanted me to hear the news firsthand." He trembled. "If she can't raise the baby on her own, can we help her?"

With one swift turn, she twirled out of his arms and stepped back. "She's not our responsibility, and neither is her kid."

"I didn't say we'd adopt the baby. I said we'd help." A choke swallowed his voice.

Help. She inhaled sharply and stared at her bare feet on the hardwood floor. What exactly did help entail when a baby was involved? Babysitting every other weekend? Endless diaper changes, interrupted sleep, and rounds of laundry from the constant spit-up and accidents? How could she cope with the stench of bodily fluids and the high-pitched wail of someone who had no words? Another wave of guilt washed over her. Maybe that's why she lost the twins. She wasn't fit to be a mother.

He touched her wrist. "Let's not talk about Michelle and her baby anymore."

Tenderness bolted through her. Not talk about Michelle and the baby. Okay, but how would not talking erase the ghosts of their presence from the corners of their home? "I'm sorry we never had kids." Geraldine sighed, her shoulders sagging. "I thought we were still happy."

"We are." He traced the curve of her arm.

Covering her face with her hands, she collapsed against him.

He kissed her forehead, her temple, her cheek, and her neck while he unzipped the dress and slipped his hands against her bare skin.

She shivered. The embers of desire sparked and flamed. Hungry for more, she dropped her hands from her face and sought his mouth, the memory of loss temporarily forgotten in the haze of pleasure tingling across her skin. She plunged deeper into passion, no longer imaging herself as Lionel's Golden Goddess but as Elliot's pretty lady.

Chapter Eleven

After another hot and sweaty softball practice, Lionel joined his teammates for drinks at the bar across from the park. A shock of cool air blasted from the vents. The lively chatter of the happy hour patrons bounced off the walls. The evening light hit the beveled glass in the door, casting rainbow streamers across the hardwood floor like a celebration. Groaning, Lionel took his seat between Nick and Cassidy. The muscles in his thighs and arms were sore. He wanted to go home and not celebrate. The team had lost the Western National Championships two weekends ago, which they needed to win to play for the title of World Masters in Las Vegas. "I don't know why we're even practicing anymore." Crossing his arms on the counter, he slumped.

Nick ordered a pitcher of beer and poured the glasses for his teammates. When he was finished, he gulped the foamy head of beer and patted Lionel on the back. "I can sponsor the team."

"Why would you do that?" Lionel straightened his spine and sipped from the icy mug. The bitter brew swirled in his mouth and warmed his throat.

"Doesn't matter if we can't compete for the title. We play for fun." Smiling, Nick waved a hand around the room. "None of us plays professionally."

Cassidy puffed his chest. "*I* was drafted by the

major leagues."

Chuckling, Nick almost spat out a mouthful of beer. "You didn't play."

Shaking his head, Cassidy stared at the counter. "Stephanie got pregnant. How could I leave?" He took a swallow from the mug. A slow smile spread across his face. "We had Adam. I wouldn't trade in that boy for a chance to play in the World Series."

Nick slapped a hand on the counter. "Let's take a vote." Standing, he faced the crowd of teammates hunched at the bar and tables. "I'm offering to cover all expenses to Vegas, including food, travel, and lodging, if we still want to play in the World Masters. I just need to see how many want to go. Raise your hand if your answer is yes." He glanced around the room, tallying the votes. "And how many don't want to play?" Nodding, he counted the lifted hands. Turning to Lionel, he smiled. "Looks like Vegas won."

Lionel hadn't voted. He didn't mind Nick sponsoring the trip. The guy could spend his millions anyway he wanted. Lionel just didn't care whether or not he played in the final tournament this year. He had other worries. Like Michelle's pregnancy. Already a few days had passed since her doctor's appointment, and she hadn't made a decision. He ran his fingers through his thinning white hair. Heck, she hadn't even told her boyfriend yet. Each morning, after the guy peeled into the parking lot and kissed her goodbye, she walked to the loading dock and shook her head so Lionel wouldn't even have to ask. The days were numbered—four to be exact. He cupped his palms against the condensation on the mug. He didn't want a decision made by default because of her procrastination.

"Hey, LJ, I thought you'd be happier." Nick clapped his shoulder. "An all-expenses-paid trip to Vegas and four days of softball. What could be better?"

Grunting, Lionel swiveled away to stare at the light changing through the beveled glass. When the sun lowered, the light became thinner, almost transparent, with the hint of nightfall starting at the top edges of the glass and descending almost imperceptibly. If he glanced over his shoulder an hour later, he would glimpse the entire pane of glass black with nightfall.

"Everything all right at home?"

Nick's voice sounded against his back. After turning on the stool, Lionel glanced into his friend's face. "Same as always. What about you?"

"Fine." Nick rubbed his nose with the back of his hand. "Cassidy's team has made great progress transforming that abandoned warehouse into low-income housing and a community center. Hope has been really pleased."

"I still can't believe the city council approved your plans." Lionel had dealt with the demographics and the challenges of integrating the rich and the poor when he entertained building a second store on the other side of town. "Who did you pay off?"

"No one." Nick tilted the mug and stared into the foamy remains. "I'm not like my father was."

"You know I was only teasing." Grinning, Lionel smacked his elbow.

Cassidy lifted his chin. "Speaking of teasing, how do you guys cope when your women lead you on when it comes to sex but then change their minds at the last minute?" He waved his hands. "Deb gets all dolled up in lingerie then strips it off and wears that potato-sack nightgown and curls away from me in bed, or she goes out with your wives drinking and comes back home and passes out before we make it to second base." He heaved a sigh. "Now she avoids all of my advances."

"That's your problem for marrying a nun." Lionel chuckled. "That woman thinks praying is foreplay."

Narrowing his eyes, Cassidy scratched his chin. "Hmm...I never thought of other uses for those rosary beads until now."

Lionel laughed until tears spilled. Wiping his cheeks with the back of his hand, he sobered up. "Just be patient and let her approach you."

Cassidy grumbled. "I'll be waiting until Christmas."

Nick raised a hand and counted on his fingers. "September, October, November, December. Only four months away."

"My hand will be tired by then."

Everyone laughed.

Buoyed by the banter, Lionel missed the ping from his cell phone. When he plunged his hand into his pocket to pay for his portion of the drinks, he caught his breath at the blinking green light on his cell phone. Swiping his finger across the screen, he read the cryptic message from Michelle.

—*I told him.*—

A cold shudder ripped through him. He tossed a twenty-dollar bill on the counter.

Cassidy glanced at the tiny screen. "What's wrong?"

Shaking his head, Lionel squeezed the phone against his chest. "Nothing." A flush of heat rushed to his face.

Nick playfully punched Cassidy's shoulder. "His wife sent a dirty picture."

"Very funny." Cassidy faked a laugh. "You guys sure know how to rub salt in the wound, don't you?" He stood and grabbed his cap. "See you at the next practice."

After handing the bartender his credit card, Nick stood and handed Lionel the twenty. "Keep it. You've paid for enough rounds this season."

Grumbling, Lionel shoved the bill into his pocket. He waited until after the two men left before he lowered his phone and typed.

—*What did he say?*—

He gripped the phone in his sweaty palm and listened to his jagged breathing while he waited for her to respond. The beveled glass transformed from blue to violet to black before he tucked the unanswered question into his pocket and drove home, wondering what would happen next.

****

Geraldine lay in bed, watching the end of the ten o'clock news with Noelle curled by her feet. When the garage door *click-clacked* and the truck's engine rumbled, she sat and fluffed the pillows behind her back and smoothed the satin nightgown over her legs.

Minutes later, Lionel emerged from the hallway, a halo of light surrounding him.

"What took you so long, sugar?" She had spent a good portion of the evening waiting for him to come home and eat dinner with her, but by the time nine o'clock rolled around, she abandoned the idea. Heating up fried chicken and mashed potatoes in the microwave, she ate standing over the kitchen sink, watching the shadows of the trees and plants waver against the dark sky. The last hour she spent staring at the flickering images of the TV, wondering where he was and what he was doing. Twice, she typed out a text and erased the message, not wanting to come across as angry or sullen, preferring to lie in bed and ignore the situation until the silence gnawed at her insides. She stroked the length of Noelle's back with her foot. "I thought practice ended at eight."

"We stopped at the bar across the street for a pitcher of beer." He flicked off the hall light and closed the bedroom door. After grabbing the remote, he switched off the TV and sank on the edge of the bed to remove his shoes and socks.

Noelle stood and trotted to his side of the bed.

Glancing at the dog, he smiled. "You miss your daddy?" He scratched behind her ear.

"What did you guys talk about?" Geraldine slid beneath the covers.

"Nick wants to sponsor the team to go to Vegas to play in the World Masters for fun." He guffawed. "I really don't give a damn anymore. I can't bat for shit."

Hmm...he used to be so happy just to play. His joints must be killing him. She touched his shoulder. "Don't beat yourself up, sugar."

Shrugging off her hand, he stood, unbuckled his belt, and slid off his pants.

He checked his phone. The screen glowed with a soft blue light, illuminating the deep frown lines framing his lips.

Sensing his frustration, she tensed. "What's wrong, sugar?"

Glancing up, he stared mutely before he bent to plug the phone into the charger on the nightstand. "I got a text from Michelle. She told her boyfriend about the baby. When I asked for his response, she didn't text back." Lying beneath the covers, he crossed his arms behind his head. "I'm worried about her."

The tenderness in his voice sent an ache through her. Why did he send a text to Michelle but not her? She sighed, struggling to brush aside the negative thought and focus on the present situation. "Oh, sugar, she probably switched off her phone and went to sleep." She leaned over and kissed his salty lips. "Get some rest. You'll see her tomorrow."

Uncurling his arms from behind his head, he nestled her against his chest and kissed her forehead. "I can't shake the feeling something is wrong."

She shuddered, registering his concern. "Sometimes I think you care more about that girl than you care about me."

"Don't be ridiculous." He hugged her tighter. "She's a kid. You're my wife."

Nestling her ear against his chest, she listened to the rise and fall of his breath and the *tick-tick-ticking* of his heart. Was he speaking the truth? Did he love her more? "You missed dinner."

After a long pause, he sighed. "I'm sorry."

"I made fried chicken, your favorite." She blinked, and her throat tightened. Rubbing her fingers back and forth across his shirt, she breathed in the scent of grass and perspiration. The sour smell of beer leaked through his pores. She closed her eyes, hoping to sleep.

He rubbed her shoulder through the satin nightgown that slid against her skin. "I should have called."

"Yes, you should have." She exhaled, and her eyelids fluttered open.

"I'm not perfect. I already said I'm sorry."

The sharp edge to his voice startled her. For a moment, she jerked awake, more aware than she had been all day. Of course, she didn't expect him to be perfect. But what type of man neglected his wife? Somehow, she expected better behavior. "I know you're sorry."

"Then why can't you forgive me?"

She swallowed. After slipping her hand beneath his shirt, she traced the hairs in the valley between his chest and his groin.

He gripped her hand, pressing her palm flat against his warm stomach.

What was there to forgive? He could not stop his concern for Michelle any more than she could stop the loop of expectations from repeating in her mind. The narratives ran parallel to each other, never intersecting, and never getting the actual story right. But what could she do? What could either of them do? She tugged free her hand and rolled away to face the moonlit window. Tucking a hand beneath her cheek, she sighed. "I do forgive you." The lie fell like a pebble from her lips.

Chapter Twelve

When Lionel entered the loading dock the next morning, he expected to hear the peel of tires against asphalt and the soft click of the passenger door before Michelle stepped out of her boyfriend's car for work. He wanted to rush over, fold her in his arms, and ask if everything was all right. But by the time the sun burned off the fog and the first delivery truck drove up to the dock, she had not arrived.

Glancing at the clock on the wall above the employee lounge, he tensed his jaw. She was exactly one hour and fifty-two minutes late. He stepped aside while the delivery man unloaded cases of beer into the stockroom and, with trembling fingers, located her phone number. Without ringing, the phone flipped over to voice mail. Without listening to her solemn voice asking him to leave a message, he hit the end call button. A bundle of nerves knotted in his stomach. He was the only one at the store, but he needed to leave as soon as he signed the delivery slip. Who could he call?

At this hour, Geraldine was most likely either lying in bed or standing in the shower or walking Noelle around the block.

He paced the length of the warehouse. If he was lucky, she might have risen early. If he called, he might catch her standing in the kitchen and gazing out the window with a cup of steaming black coffee between her palms. She might thank him for letting her know he needed her to come to work early so he could leave and find Michelle, or she might reprimand him and accuse him of loving the employee more than the wife. He strode another lap around the warehouse. Damned if he did call; damned if he didn't call. Bowing his head, he rubbed the sweat off his furrowed brow.

What alternatives did he have? Sighing, he clasped his hands behind his back. He could call Hope, and ask her to come with him to the reservation, and he could call Jeffrey, and ask him to trade hours. He would return to the store long before nightfall, early enough to cover the dinner shifts and the closing hours. Yes, that plan sounded solid.

"Sign here, sir." The delivery man handed him an electronic tablet and pen.

Without verifying the case count, Lionel scribbled his signature.

After the delivery truck rumbled out of the parking lot, Lionel closed the loading dock, strolled over to the employee lounge, and sat in a chair to make the first call. As soon as he heard Jeffrey's voice, he stumbled forward. "There's been an emergency—nothing wrong with Geraldine or Noelle—and I need to leave immediately. Can we trade shifts? Thanks. I appreciate it. See you in a few minutes." He stood and paced the length of the room to make the second call.

The phone rang three times before Hope answered. "I was wondering when I'd hear from you."

He shifted the phone to his other ear and clenched his jaw. The lack of a formal greeting grated on his nerves. If he didn't need permission to enter the reservation, he would not have called the witchy woman. He would have gone alone. After all, he had Michelle's address. Everything about her was contained in her employee file. He huffed. "I need your help."

"Of course, you do. You're like most men who don't listen to wisdom. You get yourself into jams and need someone to get you out."

"I'm not in a jam." He lifted one arm, his hand balled into a fist. "I need to find Michelle. She didn't come to work. She's not answering her phone. I think she might be in trouble." He exhaled and lowered his arm, tucking it across his chest. He shoved his cold fingers into the warm armpit. "I need permission to enter the reservation and see if she's home."

"What if I don't give you permission?" Hope raised her voice. "What if I go alone?"

"You can't." He bowed his head, and his voice broke. "She doesn't know you. She trusts me."

"All right, we'll compromise."

A big breath of air released from his lungs, and he smiled. "Thank you, Hope."

"Don't thank me yet. You haven't heard what I'm proposing."

Damn woman, learning negotiating tactics from her billionaire business husband. Standing, he strode to the sink and poured a glass of water to lubricate his parched throat. "I'm listening."

"We stop by the tribal police station and let one of the officers drive us to her dwelling. If her boyfriend is home, you stay in the car and let the officer knock on the door. If she is alone, you and I will approach the home. Does that sound like an agreeable plan?"

The muscles in his jaw tightened. Why did they need to stop at the tribal police station? Why couldn't he just bring a bat, one of the hard, wooden ones he kept at the store to deter burglars, and confront the boyfriend? The phone slipped against his sweaty palm, and he switched hands, pressing the phone to his other ear. "I don't like getting the police involved."

"You're a white man on Native lands. You need the law on your side, or everything could go wrong." She cleared her throat. "The Great Spirit warned you."

He pounded a fist against the counter. "Red is a color, not a warning."

"Oh, what little you know."

"Then enlighten me, you witch." He squeezed shut his eyes. Oh, why had he tossed out the insult? He needed her. "I'm sorry. I didn't mean to offend you."

"No offense taken. I understand you white people don't know the difference between a shaman and a madman." She paused. "So, do we have an agreement or not?"

He placed his palm against his chest, as if the gesture alone could quiet his hammering heartbeat. "Yes, we do. Where shall we meet?"

"I'll be by the store in a half hour."

When the call ended, he slumped against the counter and buried his head in his arms. He still had not called Geraldine to let her know his plans. Maybe he wouldn't. He already had too much on his plate. He didn't need her petty jealousy interfering with his mission to rescue Michelle from whatever darkness she had entered and lead her and the baby into the safety of light.

****

Dressed in her silky kimono, Geraldine stood on the deck next to Noelle, watching the golden fingers of sunlight comb through the misty fog and dab the first rays of warmth against her face and shoulders. In one hand, she cupped her mug of steaming black coffee. In the other hand, she held her phone. Since the advent of technology, she carried a phone as an extension of her arm except during sleep. As a business owner, she always expected a call. Someone needed a schedule change or a last-minute favor. Even on those days when Lionel arrived early and she stayed late, she received a handful of calls from employees who trusted her goodwill and sound judgment over Lionel's, who seemed almost indifferent to their needs...except for Michelle.

Muscles tightened in her lower back. She didn't know why Lionel was so fascinated by her. She hadn't seen him obsessed with anyone or anything since they fell in love in high school. Biting the inside of her mouth, she worried he might be falling into a midlife crisis and wondered how she might rescue him from slipping over the abyss.

She set her phone and coffee mug on the railing of the deck and stooped to smell the morning glories, azaleas, and hydrangeas in their pots. She loved the mornings she could linger in the backyard, enjoying the fruits of her labor and the quiet stillness of dawn. The twitter of the birds punctuated the silence like snippets of music. Standing, she stretched and yawned, feeling the delicious release of tension.

On the railing, her phone rang.

With her long manicured fingers, she picked up the phone and swiped her finger across the screen to answer the call. "Good morning, sugar."

"GG," Lionel's voice barreled down the line. "I

need to let you know I've switched hours with Jeffrey."

A rush of noise crackled over the line. Frowning, she touched the collar of her kimono. She had been looking forward to their dinner reservations with Nick and Hope to discuss the details of the World Masters tournament. "But tonight, we have plans—"

"Oh, no, I'm sorry."

His remorse languished between them, as thick as a blanket of fog, the same as last night.

"We'll reschedule," he promised. "I have an emergency."

With her knees buckling, she sank into a lounge chair.

Noelle buried her snout in her outstretched hand.

"Are you at the hospital?"

"No, Hope and I are driving—"

"Why are you with Hope? Is Nick all right?" Shaking her head, she struggled to make sense of this conversation.

"Nick's fine." He exhaled. "We're headed to the reservation. Michelle never showed up for work. I called, and no one answered. I'm worried something bad has happened."

Squinting, she stroked the back of Noelle's head and scratched behind the ears. "She's probably suffering from morning sickness and can't get to the phone." Why did he care so much about that girl? A damp chill settled on her exposed skin, and she straightened the slippery kimono around her legs. When she was pregnant with the twins, she stayed in bed until noon on the days her nausea lingered. He had to open the store by himself and hire another employee to take care of the lunch rush. A spike of bitterness jolted her.

Oh, how he grumbled about the inconvenience and the expense. Leaning forward, she gritted her teeth. "Don't you remember those days?"

"How can I forget? I lived them."

"You watched." The words flung out like punches. "You weren't sick. You didn't throw up. You didn't gain weight and feel tired all the time like a beached whale."

"I did more than watch. I participated. I made you breakfast in bed, even when you couldn't eat. I worked two shifts at the store, so you could rest."

The urgency of his words pummeled her. She ducked to avoid the truth.

"Damn it, GG, I would have carried them if I could." He hitched a breath. "I would have been careful. I wouldn't have lost them."

Gasping and sputtering, she loosened her grip and almost dropped the phone. A dizzying weightlessness plunged through her stomach. Did he just accuse her of killing their babies? "I did everything the doctor recommended."

"*After* the babies were endangered." He sobbed. "You acted too late. That's why we lost them."

His voice trailed off, lost in the rumble of the wind. She straightened her spine. How dare he blame her for the early delivery?

"No one gave a damn how I felt losing those babies. Everyone only cared about you." He raised his voice. "You. You. You. Everything was about you. I was forgotten."

Was he finished talking? Or would he start up again? Blaming her for things over which she had no control. She stood and paced along the length of the deck. Now she understood why he cared so much about Michelle and her pregnancy. "You can't relive your life through other people, Lionel James Jones."

"Don't talk to me like I'm Tanya or Tony."

Stunned to hear him speak the names of their dead children, she stopped walking and leaned against the railing. Slowly, she uncurled her fingers. "She's not your wife. She's not having your baby. She's not your daughter. She's just an employee." She hoped her calm and steady voice emphasized the logic. "Don't you see how ridiculous you're behaving?"

"I'm not being ridiculous. I'm being concerned."

Concerned? Anger and jealousy ratcheted in her throat. She hoped her words would scald like boiling water on his ears. "You shouldn't be concerned unless you're having an affair with her, and she is pregnant with your child."

"How dare you accuse me of something your father did?"

At least, her father got rid of the evidence, paying for an abortion and sending the girl to work at a different store in another city. She crossed an arm over her waist and lifted her chin. "How dare you accuse me of killing our babies?"

Noelle whimpered, curling up by her feet.

Glancing down, Geraldine clutched a hand to the softness of her breasts. Noelle was their baby, too. She had replaced the twins with her constant companionship. Geraldine straightened her lips. But Noelle wasn't pregnant with a litter. She didn't need him like Michelle did.

"I am *not* your father," Lionel said. "I'm not having an affair with Michelle. She's like a daughter to me."

She huffed, unclenching the hand at her breasts and curling it around the railing of the deck. "That's the problem, sugar. She's *not* your daughter. Leave her alone." Tired of his obsession bordering on madness, she decided not to tolerate it any longer. "I love you, but I don't approve of your actions. You need to come back. Let Hope deal with that woman. You're needed here, at home and at the store, not on the reservation with a girl who's practically a stranger."

"She's not a stranger," he said. "She told the doctor I was her uncle."

Oh, my goodness, the girl had roped him up in the drama, which gave Geraldine one more reason not to like her. "I don't care if she lied to the doctor. You are *not* her uncle. You're her employer. Now, come back. We have a business to run."

A *click* followed by an expanse of silence hissed across the line.

Either he had hung up or the line had been disconnected. She dropped her arms, the phone hot and slippery in her grasp, and gazed at Noelle still curled by her feet. A cold realization climbed through her body.

She had lost him.

Chapter Thirteen

Lionel dropped the cell phone in his lap and leaned his head against the passenger's window. "I'm sorry you had to hear that conversation."

Turning onto a dirt road, Hope shrugged. "I had a long-term marriage, too. We had our share of fights."

"We've been fighting a lot more lately." Lionel rubbed his forehead and squeezed his eyes shut. The air-conditioning blasted cold air against his skin. As the tires rumbled over the unpaved road, the car rocked his body back and forth. Opening his eyes, he stared out at the dense woods. "GG doesn't understand why I'm concerned about Michelle. She's young. She's pregnant. She's scared." He sighed. "I want to help her like a father would."

Nodding, she steered toward a clearing. "The Wapi have a saying, 'All time is now.' You are reliving your past while you are steeped in the present. Both experiences are real and immediate." She paused. "I understand your grief is endless. I felt that same way after losing Richard."

Gaping, he shifted in his seat. "How did you get through the loss?"

She kept her gaze focused on the road, her hands on the wheel, her breath steady and strong, but a tremor released.

The energy was so palpable he could feel its rays

penetrate his skin.

"For a long time, I didn't. When I met Nick, he taught me how to let go." She met his gaze and smiled. "He had worked through his father's death years ago, so he knew the landscape in which I traveled. He waited until I stopped waking up crying for a man who had died. I chose a new life, and I was at peace."

Shaking his head, he could not imagine the relief of letting go of his grief over losing the twins. He could not imagine glimpsing a baby without feeling that tug in his chest. He could not imagine letting Michelle go.

Hope drove into the parking lot of the tribal police station and shut off the engine. "Stay here." She rolled down the windows halfway before she stepped out of the vehicle.

The warm scent of pines and redwoods floated on the light breeze. The police station wasn't anything remarkable—just a whitewashed shack with a sign next to the window and a squad car parked on the other side of the makeshift lot. The poverty of the place amazed him. With millions of dollars of profits from the casino each year, why couldn't the tribe pave the parking lot and renovate the police station?

A few minutes later, Hope returned. She opened the passenger door and waved toward the squad car. "We're riding with Wild Bird."

The man named Wild Bird stepped out of the station, squinting into the morning light. He wore his long hair braided against his back, his white-and-black uniform was as wrinkled as if he had fallen asleep in it, and dust covered the black shoes on his feet. He was fairly young, at least under forty, and had that air of nonchalance easily mistaken for indolence. "Officer

Wild Bird." He stuck out a dark hand.

Lionel shook the man's greasy palm and followed him to the squad car. Following instructions, he took a seat in the back against the warm leather.

Hope and Wild Bird sat in the front.

Lionel read Michelle's address from the scrap of paper tucked into his pocket.

Wild Bird started the engine and backed out of the lot.

The car had no air-conditioning, and the wind whipping into the cab was too thin and warm to be refreshing. Lionel stared out the window at the recurring scenery—rows of trees followed by patches of clearings dotted with a few shacks. The vision of poverty struck him with the same force he had experienced traveling to Honduras to swim with the dolphins on his twenty-fifth wedding anniversary. The winding, two-lane roads cut through jungles of tropical trees with an occasional wooden shanty rising like a small mountain. Children darkened by sunlight and dirt squatted on the crumbling decks. Each time he stared into their eyes, he winced from his stomach tightening over the chronic neglect.

Turning into a clearing, Wild Bird parked the vehicle.

When Lionel recognized Paul's sports car parked in front of the shack, he tensed his jaw. He wanted to lurch out of the back seat, stomp to the front door, and demand Paul release Michelle.

Hope glanced over her shoulder and caught his stare. "You stay here."

"I can't." He swallowed.

She touched his hand. "Keep a low profile. You

don't need to be seen. You'll only cause more trouble."

"If that bastard is keeping her hostage—"

"Then we'll take care of it." Hope spun toward the tribal police officer. "Won't we, Wild Bird?"

Without a word, Wild Bird glanced into the rearview mirror and nodded.

Hope drifted out of the car with her caftan dress blowing against her ankles to meet Wild Bird in his rumpled uniform at the front door. After Wild Bird knocked three times, Paul opened the door and peered from one face to the other before cutting his gaze over to the squad car.

Lionel ducked, lying low against the warm seat that smelled of old leather and dying, and squeezed shut his eyes and his hands closed. He didn't want to lock stares with a man he wanted to beat to death. Several moments later, feet scuffled on the deck, and the front door clicked shut. Peering between the front seats, he glanced across the empty yard to the curtained windows like eyes swollen shut in a battered face. With every breath, his heartbeat ticked upward. Helplessness cloaked him as he hunched in the backseat, the same helplessness that anchored him to the chair beside GG who lay on a hospital bed with a fetal monitor hooked up to the peak of her abdomen. He stared at the shack with the same intense interest as he had studied the tiny screen with its jagged white lines recording the fluctuating rhythm of two sets of heartbeats.

He wanted to leap from the car and storm the house, just like he had wanted to rip off the tubes hooked to his wife and carry her home. But he stayed in the backseat, lying outside the vision of anyone surrounding him, just like he had sat speechlessly when the doctor and nurse arrived and wheeled his wife out of the room for an emergency C-section to deliver the twins twelve weeks before they were due. The creak of the wind through the branches sounded like the cries of newborns in the hospital rooms along the corridor. He waited for Hope and Wild Bird to return with Michelle just like he had waited for the doctor to return with his wife and the twins.

When the driver's door opened, Lionel lurched upright, eyes wide.

Wild Bird slid into the car and shook his head. "The girl's fine. She was sleeping, that's all."

"Where's Hope?" He leaned toward the front seat, glancing at the house.

Wild Bird gestured for him to lie down. "Don't worry. She wanted to talk to the girl."

Stretched out against the cracked leather that stank of sweat, he clutched his twisting stomach. "I can't believe you left her alone."

"I have no need to protect her. She is a medicine woman. The Great Spirit watches over her always."

"Then why did we come here with you?"

Wild Bird glanced into the rearview mirror and smiled. "I'm here for the boy. To let him know he is not above the law."

Groaning, Lionel closed his eyes and waited.

Minutes later, the passenger door opened, and Hope slipped inside.

Lionel struggled to sit.

Shaking her head, she flashed a warning glance.

Lionel lay on the seat, feeling every divot in the road the tires jolted across from the poor suspension. The rocking only pitched a wave of nausea, and he clutched his stomach, hoping he wouldn't throw up in the squad car.

"You can sit up now," Wild Bird said.

Slowly, Lionel propped himself up. The roiling in his gut subsided when he planted his feet on the mat. "What happened?"

"She overslept." Hope glanced over her shoulder. "I told her to rest. She'll be at work tomorrow. I also asked her to transfer her medical file to the tribal clinic. They can take better care of her here."

Laughing, Lionel pointed to the rickety buildings they passed. "Does the clinic even have a fetal monitor?"

Hope narrowed her gaze. "She'll be with her people."

"What about the baby?" He lifted his arms. "Don't you want the baby to have the best care?"

"Of course, I do. But she'll receive the best care here, not in some impersonal, white man's medical center."

Slumping against the seat, he rolled back his head and stared at a tear in the ceiling. Everything in the reservation was dated, falling apart, or neglected. How could he trust Michelle's health and the baby's safety under those conditions?

"You need to listen to Spirit Walk." Wild Bird drove into the parking lot of the tribal police station and shut off the engine. "Our medicine woman has divine knowledge."

Groaning, Lionel shook his head. "Spirit Walk is just another one of my wife's crazy friends. She's not a medical professional."

Wild Bird nodded. "Listen to her."

Every muscle in Lionel's body collapsed. Why was he always powerless when the problems lodged themselves into women's wombs? He slapped his thighs. "I guess Michelle will make the final decision, won't she?" He opened the door and stepped outside, breathing in the fresh air.

Hope unlocked the doors of her SUV. "Let's go. I need to get you back to the store before the lunch rush."

"I'm not ready." Kicking dirt with the tip of his shoe, Lionel shoved his hands into his pockets and wondered if he could run back to Michelle's shack and ask her what the hell was going on.

"You can't stay here." She slipped into the vehicle and started the engine.

He wasn't anticipating the long, monotonous ride back to the store with Hope beside him, nagging him to let go, to move onward, and to shed the last twenty years of grief as quickly as one sheds twenty pounds. But he couldn't stay here with Wild Bird eyeing him. And he couldn't run fast enough to get away from a squad car. Opening the door, he slid inside and tugged the seat belt across his waist. He stared out the window, knowing the questions he wanted to ask had no answers because Hope hadn't bothered to ask Michelle what he really wanted to know.

Chapter Fourteen

The service bell rang. Geraldine lifted her head, and the muscles in her hands froze in the middle of swiping mayonnaise over white bread. How dare Lionel enter the store as if nothing had happened? Swallowing bitter saliva, she glowered.

At the checkout line, Lionel tied an apron around his waist and waved for Jeffrey to take a lunch break. He slipped behind the cash register and greeted the next customer with a smile.

What a coward. Ice flushed through her body, numbing everything. How dare he ignore her after the fight they had on the phone. If he was brave, he would have cut across the deli line for a kiss and hug, telling her he was sorry, he had overreacted, and he didn't need to parent some wayward teen to feel like a real man. But from the way he avoided her, he was afraid she might confront and embarrass him in public, raising her voice, commanding attention, and making the scene as gossip-worthy as the daytime soap operas most of their customers watched.

Forget him. She tucked her chin toward her chest and focused on arranging the salami and provolone on the sandwich she was making. When she finished, she handed the packaged sandwich to the customer and waved to the next person in line.

After preparing three different sandwiches, she fell

into a rhythm—spread, stack, wrap. The comfort of monotony soothed her. When she was little and her parents fought, she would escape into the kitchen and make sandwiches—elaborate concoctions of whatever was available in the fridge. Some of those experiments were edible; the rest were given to the dog. Over time, she learned what people enjoyed. By the time she was sixteen and employed at the deli, her sandwiches became the most desired meal in town.

"Well, well, well…how are you today, my pretty lady?"

The accented voice poured over her head and shoulders and coated her body. Glancing up, she stared into Elliot's meadow-green eyes. She breathed in his scent of bergamot and oranges. He never stank of hard work and perspiration like Lionel did.

Elliot leaned against the counter. "I thought I'd enjoy one of your sandwiches today."

"You want the pastrami on rye with everything on it like last time, or do you want to try something different?" She flashed a smile, holding his gaze for a second longer.

"I'll try the ham and cheese on sourdough with everything on it." He winked.

"Coming right up." She dropped two pieces of sourdough bread into the toaster. Staring at her husband across the store, she willed him to meet her gaze.

Lionel continued to ignore her, his head dipped low, counting out change into a customer's hand.

Crossing her arms over her chest, she fumed. Didn't he know she needed a shared moment of intimacy?

"What's bothering you, pretty lady?"

With a quick swivel of her head, she regained her focus.

Elliot stared, an eyebrow divot wrinkling his forehead.

Softness melted her shoulders. Why did he care? He hardly knew her. "I'm good, sugar."

"I know you're good." He swept his gaze from her chest toward her crown. "I'm wondering what's on your mind."

Heaving a sigh, she removed the two slices of bread and set them on the counter. She didn't want to confide in anyone about her growing list of personal problems. "What are you planning to do today?"

"Well, now that you ask, I was hoping you might tell me what a newcomer should do."

She stacked the ham and cheese on one slice of bread and everything else on the other. "You need to visit the Wapi Museum. We have the greatest collection of Native American artifacts in Northern California." She folded the slices together and cut the sandwich in half. "If you like wine tasting, we have plenty of tour guides to take you on several different routes. If you like food, you should go visit the dairy. They give out the best samples of cheese and ice cream." After wrapping the sandwich with butcher paper, she taped the package shut. "If you like shopping, there are a ton of designer boutiques along the square."

"Thanks, pretty lady." As he grabbed the sandwich, he brushed his fingers across her knuckles. "What would you recommend I do with you?"

Pleasure traveled up her arm, and her whole body rushed with heat.

"Oh, you won't be doing anything with me." She

frowned. "I'm working 'til five." She thought a second longer. "Lionel and I had dinner plans with friends that had to be canceled because he switched shifts with an employee."

"So, you're free tonight?" He tilted his head.

"Yes, technically, I am." A slow smile spread across her face. "What are you suggesting?"

"Do you like Irish stew?"

Didn't the Irish have boring, bland food? Or was that stereotype about the British? She wiped her hands on a dish towel. At least, she wouldn't have to cook. More importantly, she wouldn't be alone. She could feed and walk Noelle and arrive home before Lionel climbed into bed around ten. No one would know she had dinner with Elliot. She shifted her weight to one hip. "I don't know. I've never tried it."

He fumbled in his pocket and found a pen. After tugging a napkin from the dispenser on the counter, he wrote his name, number, and address. "Come over at seven, and we'll share what's leftover." He handed her the information.

The warmth of his smile wrapped around her shoulders and tugged her close. She tucked the scribbled-on napkin into the front pocket of her apron and waved goodbye. "See you tonight, sugar."

"Looking forward, pretty lady." He winked.

A dance of heat tingled from her scalp to the soles of her feet. Turning to the next customer, she brightened her smile. "What can I get you today, sugar?"

While the customer rattled off the order, she listened, touching the soft bulge in her apron where the napkin dwelled, safe and hidden from the rest of the world.

****

Fading evening light highlighted the brass knocker on the front door of Elliot's townhome. Geraldine remembered when this little subdivision had been built. She and Lionel had been house hunting, but they couldn't afford the model they liked best—with four bedrooms, two-and-a-half bathrooms, and cathedral ceilings. Each month, they kept searching, as the pregnancy progressed, until they found a converted barn just minutes from Larry's Deli. The two upstairs bedrooms overlooked an open field and the downstairs included a formal dining room, a full bathroom, and a garage. Geraldine believed they would sell and purchase something larger as their family grew, but after losing the twins, they decided to stay.

Dressed in a summer dress with spaghetti straps and kitten heels, she clutched her favorite purse against her hip and rubbed her lips together before ringing the doorbell.

A few seconds later, Elliot flung wide the door and smiled. With one sweeping arm gesture, he waved her inside. "Welcome to my humble home, pretty lady."

She stepped into the narrow hall, her heels *click-clacking* against the parquet flooring and rounded the corner into the quaint kitchen with a small table surrounded by four chairs, an oak hutch filled with china and knickknacks, and a stove bubbling with the warm smells of simmering lamb and potatoes. She raised an eyebrow. "Do you need any help?"

Shaking his head, he pulled back a chair. "Be seated. I'll pour the wine." He lifted two bottles. "Red or white?"

"Red, please." After taking a seat at the table, she set her purse on one of the other chairs. She shifted on the chair, suddenly uncomfortable sitting in another man's kitchen while he cooked. When Lionel served dinner, he arranged takeout on their fine china. He didn't know how to cook from a recipe. Over the years they had been together, he had never learned.

"Cheers." Elliot perched on the closest chair and offered a toast.

She clicked her glass against his and sipped the full-bodied wine. "What are we celebrating?"

When he chuckled, he lit up—the skin around his twinkling eyes crinkled and the smattering of freckles across his cheeks danced across his skin. "Life, my pretty lady, what else is there to celebrate?"

She would drink to that sentiment. He always made her feel alive. "So, tell me about yourself."

After setting the glass on the table, he stood and filled two bowls with stew. He placed one bowl before her and the other by him. Next, he carried a basket full of bread and butter. "Not homemade, I'm afraid. But the bakery across the street does a lovely job. I always take a wedge and use it as a spoon." He arranged the basket between them and sat. Bowing his head, he made the sign of the cross and silently prayed.

Recognizing the gesture, she leaned forward. "Are you Catholic?"

He nodded. "Lifelong, I believe. Though, of course, I can't remember much before I was four. And you?"

Shaking her head, she frowned. "No affiliation. I think I'm more agnostic than atheist. Most of my friends believe in something."

He dipped his bread into the stew and took a hearty bite. When he was finished, he lifted his glass and sipped. "So, you want to know a bit about me." He winked. "I'm not much of a storyteller, so I'll stick with the facts. I was born and raised in Ireland. Married my childhood sweetheart, Nancy, when I was just a lad of twenty, and we had a daughter, Sharon, a few years later. About three years ago, Nancy died from lymphoma." A mist passed over his eyes. "Sharon had already left for work in London, and I felt no need to stay. I wanted to start over, so I came here."

Compassion spread throughout her body. "I had no idea you were married with a family." She lowered her slice of bread into the stew. The sobering details of his life stripped away her fantasy of a carefree single man owning a bar in a small Northern California town. He was just as mangled by love as the rest of the people she knew. She bit into the bread and tasted the onion and the bullion in the doughy softness. "Why did you choose Vine Valley? Why not New York or Los Angeles?"

"My wife always wanted to start a winery here. She read about it in some travelogue while she was sick. I promised I would make her dream come true as soon as she recovered." With the bread, he sopped another mouthful of stew. "When she died, I toyed around with the idea for a couple of years, but I couldn't find the heart to embark on that type of adventure without her." Dropping his head, he stared into the stew. "But when the grief lingered, I decided I couldn't stay in Ireland, either. Everything reminded me of her. So, I told Sharon I was moving to Vine Valley, California. She cried and asked me why so far away when I would always carry Mom here." He pointed to his chest. "I told her I needed a fresh start where no one knew me, and I knew no one."

Bowing her head, she breathed in the steaming aroma of the chunky stew and wondered if he had used Nancy's recipe. If she died before Lionel, would he learn how to cook, fumbling with the measuring spoons and all those foreign spices? "I'm so sorry for your loss." She squeezed his hand.

He snuggled close and parted her lips with a sudden kiss.

The shock of his tongue in her mouth sent her head spinning. She plunged into a dark and wild ocean, waves of lust crashing against her floundering body. Stumbling to find her center, she jerked back and stiffened, yanking her fingers out of his grasp. "I'm happily married."

"Are you?" He scooted toward the edge of his chair, his knee wedged against her thigh. "Then why the long face?"

She couldn't remember the last time another man kissed her. The delightful fantasy she imagined clashed with the reality of a foreign taste and a strange touch. How could she cross the same line her father crossed after promising herself she would never be like him? She glanced away. Heat drained from her skin. After shoving back the chair, she fumbled for her purse.

"Do you really want to walk out right now and lose the little bit of fun in your life?"

She clutched her purse to her chest and wiggled on the chair. Her heartbeat thudded against her hands, and she gulped a mouthful of air. Oh, why had she believed she could stop flirting before the kiss?

"Please stay, pretty lady." He placed a hand on her thigh, separating her legs.

A rush of warmth flooded her, and she dropped her purse.

Bending, he plucked the strap and set the purse on the chair beside her. He slid his hand farther up her thigh, his fingers pressing against the moistness of her panties.

She gasped. How could she leave without creating a scene?

"How does this feel?" He slid the strap of her dress over her shoulder and dotted kisses from the nape of her neck to the curve of her breast. With one hand massaging between her legs, he flicked his tongue back and forth across a nipple until it hardened like a tiny nut.

Tipping back her head, she grabbed his closely shorn hair and groaned. Oh, how did Elliot know how to make her feel so good?

He slid his fingers beneath her panties and slipped inside the warm, wet tunnel.

A whimper escaped her lips.

Thrusting his fingers, he gripped her close and kissed her neck. When the pressure mounted, he trailed away, his fingers stroking the sides. As soon as the tension slackened, he strummed deeper.

At his playing her body like a song, she quivered. "I can't." She panted against the mounting pleasure, her body sinking under the weight of desire. If she stayed any longer, she risked going under and drowning. With one last gasp, she shuddered.

He withdrew his fingers and, with his lips, found her mouth again. Slipping one arm around her shoulders and the other arm under her hips, he hoisted her into his arms and carried her up the stairs, down a hallway, and into the light of his bedroom where he shut the door with a foot and tossed her on the mattress.

With the length of his hot, firm body against her, she floated on her back, her face, her arms, and her legs drowning from the weight of his body.

"I want to come inside you." He stood, unbuckled his belt, and wriggled out of his pants.

Glancing at his hard, glistening body, she could not imagine how he would feel moving inside her. "I've only been with Lionel." As soon as she spoke her husband's name, she felt his presence in the room, as palpable as her breath. What would he say if he knew she was with another man? How would he feel knowing she strayed because he could no longer give her what she needed? She shuddered, weighed down by the unbearable pain of disappointing her husband. "I'm sorry. I have to go." She rolled off the bed and stood on wobbly legs, adjusting the straps of her dress and smoothing her skirt. "I can't betray him."

He circled the bed, naked.

Raising a hand, she closed her eyes. "Please. Get dressed. Let me go."

With his hand, he cupped her chin. "I won't hurt you."

His fingers smelled like her. Breathing in the stench of betrayal, she blinked open her eyes. "That might be true, but I will hurt him." She tottered on trembling knees. Oh, how did she let herself get into so much trouble? Was she no better than her father? Shame powered through her, and she yanked her body free. After stalking around him, she headed out the bedroom door, down the stairs, and into the kitchen. She grabbed her purse and strode toward the front door.

"Wait, pretty lady."

She spun, glancing at his clothed body, the shirt askew around the collar, the buckle on his belt still undone. In the unflattering light of betrayal, he was nothing more than a pathetic middle-aged man. How could she have found him attractive? She gripped the doorknob, ready to escape. "Yes?"

He took a step forward. Lines crinkled his forehead. "Talk to me. Tell me what is wrong."

She met his softened gaze. What part didn't he understand? "I've been married to the same man for over thirty years. I've never cheated on him until tonight."

"We weren't cheating. We were having a bit of fun."

She guffawed. "You call what we were doing a 'bit of fun'?" Narrowing her gaze, she frowned. "Did you have a bit of fun during your marriage?"

"Doesn't everyone?" He shrugged, lifting his arms wide.

Shaking her head, she bit her lower lip. She remembered Deb's hot shame when she confessed breaking her holy vows when she first kissed Cassidy, who had been married at the time. Were they also having a bit of fun? She sighed. All those sexual fantasies she harbored throughout the years suddenly fell flat in the baldness of reality. She lifted her chin and broadened her stance. "I'm not some hussy you picked up off the street. I'm a human being with thoughts and feelings." She released the doorknob and knocked a fist against her heart with each word. "I matter. My husband matters." She choked on a sob. "Even you matter." She waved her hand in a circle. "Sugar, this whole night has been one big mistake."

"You're a good woman—lots of spunk and fire." He gestured behind him. "Can we finish dinner?"

She tipped back her head and laughed.

"Please, stay." He lowered his voice, taking a step. "I promise I won't make any passes. I just want us to be friends."

"Friends don't take advantage of one another." Spinning, she yanked open the door and stepped into the darkening night. A chill of fog raked up her arms. She shivered, tugging her arms over her breasts. "Goodbye, Elliot." From her purse, she withdrew the napkin he had written on and tossed it at his bewildered face as he stood beneath the lintel.

When she arrived home minutes later, she peeled off her clothes and tossed them into the laundry and stepped into a hot shower, washing the scent of his body from her skin. She scrubbed the memory of his touch from her lips, her neck, her breasts, and between her legs. After she dressed, she walked Noelle. Returning to an empty house, she climbed the stairs beside the limping dog, listening to the washing machine spin and whirl. Standing on the threshold of her bedroom, she flicked on the lights and the TV. The sounds of the newscasters filled the space with their familiar banter. She rubbed her lips, still crawling from Elliot's eager kisses. Sinking on the edge of the mattress, she covered her face with both hands.

Oh, what would she tell Lionel when he arrived home?

Chapter Fifteen

Lionel stood by the kitchen window, drinking his coffee. Last night, Geraldine lay quietly in bed when he arrived home a little after ten o'clock. In the dark room, he undressed, slipped beneath the covers, and waited. She did not roll over and caress his chest through his shirt or press kisses against the stubble on his cheeks or run her foot along the length of his leg. When he woke in the middle of the night to use the bathroom, he heard her sniffling. Maybe she was coming down with a summer cold.

Dumping the dregs of his coffee into the sink, he rinsed the cup and set it in the dishwasher. He needed to call Nick today and reschedule the dinner. The World Masters was less than a month away, and the team needed to know the logistics of the trip. With slumping shoulders, he shoved his keys, wallet, and phone into his pockets. He strode up the stairs, nudged open the bedroom door, and listened to the quiet rise and fall of Noelle's breath as she curled beside Geraldine's feet. Walking around the edge of the bed, he stood before Geraldine, who stared at the window. Two silver streaks glistened on her cheeks. He knelt beside her and stroked the hair away from her face with his calloused fingers. She wasn't suffering from a summer cold; she was just suffering. "What's wrong, GG?"

She blinked, without meeting his gaze. "I—don't—

know."

Sitting back on his heels, he let his hand drift to her chin. He tilted her face until he peered into her red-rimmed eyes. "You aren't a good liar."

She cringed, tugging the sheet over her shoulder. "I never meant to hurt anyone."

"Who did you hurt?" He searched her face, seeking the answer she wouldn't give him.

Swallowing, she wrestled away her chin and closed her eyes. "I guess it doesn't matter. What's done is done. I can't change the past."

He sucked in a breath and held it. "You're talking about the twins." He dropped his hand to his lap and stared at a loose thread in the worn carpeting. "I'm sorry I'm still grieving. I don't know when I'll stop. The pain never ends." Releasing the breath, he gasped. "Logically, I know their death wasn't your fault. Something was wrong chromosomally. The doctor explained that fact years ago." He curled his hands into fists. "But I can't help what I feel."

Was she listening?

Slowly, she wiggled to a seated position against the pillows. Wrapping her arms around her knees, she met his gaze. "I'm sorry for everything." Breaking away, she glanced at the sunlight filtering through the curtains. "It won't happen again."

"Oh, that's for sure." They were too old to try for a baby. He slapped his thighs and grabbed the edge of the mattress to hoist his cumbersome weight. Prickles of sensation danced in his legs, and he stamped his feet. "Get some rest. I know you didn't sleep well last night. I'll see you later at the store."

"No, wait." She tugged on his hand. "I'll come

with you."

"But you're working later than me."

"You can pick me up when I'm done." She swung her legs over the side of the bed and wriggled her feet into slippers. "Maybe we can go to Nick and Hope's tonight."

"Okay." He grabbed his phone out of his pocket to see the time. "We'll leave in a half hour. You go shower, and I'll take care of Noelle." He bent to kiss her cheek. "Does that sound like a plan?"

She nodded, a tentative smile curling her lips. "Thanks, Lionel."

As soon as the bathroom door closed, he sank onto the mattress and stroked Noelle's back. Something was odd about Geraldine—the way she avoided his gaze, the evasiveness of her answers, the eagerness to join him. She loved her mornings alone, out on the deck surrounded by her potted plants and flowers, soaking in the beauty of the natural world before arriving in time for the lunch hour rush. What was she hiding, and why she was hiding it? Shaking away doubt, he patted Noelle's rump. "Hey, ol' girl, time to wake up. Mommy and Daddy are leaving early today."

Noelle stirred and yawned.

Standing, he helped Noelle navigate the steps from the bed. He strolled beside her, wondering how he would have felt being a daddy to someone other than a dog. When Noelle hesitated at the first step, he lifted her into his arms and carried her down the stairs. He set her on the landing, and something softened inside of him. Maybe he was reading too much into Geraldine's odd behavior. Maybe she was just remorseful for their fight yesterday and all the misery that wedged between them over the twins.

****

During the ride to the store, Lionel held Geraldine's hand. "You're cold." With a sidelong glance, he frowned. "You sure you're feeling all right?"

"I'm fine, sugar." She curled her fingers around his palm and patted the back of his hand. "Thanks for letting me come with you."

He squeezed his warmth into her hand. Maybe she had started menopause, the dreaded "change" he had heard some of his teammates talk about when they complained about their wives. Hot flashes, wild mood swings, sometimes a complete change in personality.

"Total madness," one guy said during practice. "I never know who I'm coming home to—my wife or her evil twin."

Maybe he could offer to take her to the OB/GYN and ask about some options to make life comfortable for both of them during this transition. He drove into the parking lot, glancing at the view of the open loading dock.

Michelle stuffed her purse in the employee locker.

Sweat broke on his forehead. He tugged away his hand from Geraldine and gripped the steering wheel, swinging into the closest parking slot. After stopping the engine, he released the seat belt and bolted from the truck. "Michelle!"

She glanced over her shoulder and waved.

Panting, he bounded up the steps. Pallor lingered beneath her dark skin like she hadn't slept or eaten. Remembering GG alone in the truck, he swiveled his gaze across the parking lot.

With head downcast, Geraldine dragged her feet

across the pavement.

An ache tugged in his chest. "Hey, Michelle, go upstairs into the office." He tossed her the set of keys. "I'll meet you there in a few minutes to talk."

She nodded, catching the keys and disappearing up the stairs.

Swallowing the tightness in his throat, he lumbered down the steps and wrapped an arm around his wife's shoulders. "If you're not feeling well..."

Shrugging him off, she glared. "I'm fine, sugar."

"Why don't I make you a cup of tea? You can relax while I talk with Michelle."

"About what?"

A cold flint sparked in her blue eyes. He cringed. Why did he want his wife's approval when she would never understand how he felt? Placing his hands on his hips, he broadened his stance. "I want her side of the story, not some witchy woman's interpretation of what happened yesterday."

Narrowing her gaze, she heaved a sigh. "Why can't you believe Hope when she said the girl was tired? Don't you remember how tired I was that first trimester?"

The strain in her voice broke through him. He dropped his arms. Maybe she was right. He was overreacting. "I'm sorry." He wrapped her in his arms.

She wriggled out of his embrace and stomped up the steps. "Go talk to the girl. I'll be in the deli, slicing meat." She slashed through the plastic curtain.

Damn hormones. He jammed his hands into fists and powered up the stairs to the office. The door creaked, and he stepped inside. The room smelled musty and stuffy this early in the morning. He flicked on the overhead fan and opened the window overlooking the empty fields.

Michelle sat on the chair facing the desk littered with papers, a computer, a printer, and a landline. She tracked his movements.

Her body tensed and coiled like a snake studying a potential predator. Her saucer-like brown eyes flickered between hope and doubt. Taking the seat behind the desk, he remembered being eighteen, freshly graduated from high school and heading to Vine Valley College in the fall, working part-time at the deli, and loving Geraldine with all of his heart. What would he have done if she had gotten pregnant then? He leaned forward and clasped his hands between his knees. "How are you feeling?"

She shrugged.

"Hope said you aren't eating or sleeping. Is that true?"

She glanced away. "I couldn't come to work yesterday because Paul wouldn't drive me."

"So, you weren't tired." He leaned back against the chair and crossed a foot against his knee. "What really happened after you sent me that text when you told him you were pregnant?"

She bowed her head, and the curtain of black hair shielded her face. A shudder rippled across her shoulders. "I—can't—tell—you."

He uncrossed his legs and heaved a sigh. Standing, he paced back and forth across the length of the room, stopping once to stare at the black birds drifting across the foggy sky. "You might not be able to tell the tribal police or the medicine woman, but you can tell me." Pivoting, he waited.

The hum of the computer that ran the surveillance software twenty-four hours a day filled the room with a hush.

Lifting her head, she swept the hair from her face and rubbed the back of her hand beneath her nose. "You were there?"

He knelt before her, gripping the edge of the table for balance. "I was lying in the backseat of the squad car. They wouldn't let me come to the door to see you."

She gulped, tugging on the sleeves of her shirt.

A dark purple bruise swelled and disappeared.

Frowning, he stiffened. "Did he hurt you?"

She widened her eyes. "He doesn't want the baby."

Searching for clues, he scanned her face. "What do you want?"

She blinked her eyes and glanced away. "I...don't...know."

He touched her elbow.

She flinched.

After dropping his hand to the side, he studied her. She was afraid and vulnerable, unsure of what to do and who to trust. Didn't she know he would never hurt her? "You're safe. I'll protect you." A cramp in his leg forced him to stand. "Please, tell me."

"I can't kill it." She sniffed, tucking her hands under her armpits. "I heard the heartbeat. I know it's alive." Shaking her head, she stared at the floor. "I just don't know how I can take care of a baby without him. He's everything."

Lifting his head toward the ceiling, he stared at the fan that cut through the still air. Thoughts flitted through his mind—some reasonable, others not. "You don't need him. I can help you." He swept an arm around the room. "You could move here. This is where GG and I lived when we started out." He pointed to the door behind him. "There's a kitchenette and a bathroom and closet space. I can clear out this stuff and move it someplace else, so you have a bedroom big enough for you and the baby."

She rotated her head. "What about your wife? She doesn't like me."

"Don't worry about her. She loves to help." He paced the length of the room, his mind filling with possibilities. "She'll understand if we explain the circumstances."

"What do I tell Paul?" She frowned. "He expects me to get an abortion."

"Don't tell him anything." He gripped the ledge of the window and squinted at the gray sky. "You pack whatever you want to take in your purse and stow it in your locker each day. Things you can't live without. Things I can't replace." He dropped his hands and swiveled. "When you have everything you want stored here, you don't go home with him when he comes to pick you up. Just tell me what day that is, so I can be here to support you." He shoved his hands into his pockets. "He can't make you go. I won't let him." Nodding, he gazed at her covered arms. "You're safe with me."

For a long moment, she stared. "After the tribal police left, Hope asked to speak with me alone. She said I should transfer my medical file to the clinic on the reservation and file a domestic violence report with the tribal police."

Alarm rippled through him. "Did you?"

Shaking her head, she shuddered. "I couldn't. I

didn't have any place to go."

"Now you do." He strode across the room and touched her shoulder. "You don't have to transfer your medical file, but you do need to file that report. Just wait until the moment you know you're coming here for good. That way, you won't be around when the tribal police confront him."

She clutched her stomach and rocked forward, her hair dropping over her face. "I'm so scared. I've never felt so alone."

"Ah, sweetheart, you're not alone." He bent and folded her into his arms. "I'm here. You've got me."

She nestled against him, burying her head against his shoulder.

Breathing in the scent of her skin, sour with the sweat of fear, he focused on the baby hidden deep inside her. In honor of the memory of his twins, he vowed to protect Michelle's child, no matter the cost.

Chapter Sixteen

In the uncomfortable hum of fluorescent lighting, Geraldine placed smoked ham in the feeder. The rhythmic motions of the whirring circular blade propelled her thoughts to last night. Mulling over the images of the sexual escapade, her first without Lionel, filled her with a mixture of excitement and dread. She could still taste the briny salt of Elliot's skin, the surprising swiftness of his touch, the incredible responsiveness of her body. Confusion swirled inside her. How could she betray herself and her husband by fooling around with another man?

Shame burned her face. With trembling fingers, she switched off the slicer, rinsed her hands in the sink, and splashed cold water on her cheeks. She was no better than her father, turning against the sacred wedding vows for a moment of fleeting pleasure. All of these years, she struggled to contain her flirtatious nature with much success...until last night.

The whole urgency and suddenness of Elliot's unexpected kiss replayed on the tape of her mind—how different he felt with his coarse hair cropped close to the scalp, smooth hands, and short, clean nails. How her skin tingled from his touch even after she showered and changed once she arrived home. How remorse and regret soaked through her nightgown like sweat through her pores. How she quivered with tears, unable to accept and believe what she had done.

A sudden noise broke her concentration, and she flicked her attention toward the back of the store.

Lionel and Michelle ambled side by side.

A cloud of determination surrounded them. She stiffened, dropping the dish towel on the counter and folding her arms across her chest. "Yes?"

Steeling his stance, he dropped an arm from around Michelle's shoulders. "We have some news."

"We?" She scanned the girl's blank face and settled her gaze on her husband's hard stare.

"Michelle is having the baby, but she needs some place safe to stay." He waved toward the back of the store. "I offered her the office space."

"You did?" Geraldine flung wide her arms. "Where will we put our stuff? That computer is hooked up to the cameras, and the desk is full of human resource files."

"I'll have Cassidy build a new office downstairs behind the employee break room."

Geraldine hardened her jaw. The anger and resistance she felt toward Lionel's proposition was washed away by the guilt and remorse she felt remembering Elliot's tongue slipping down the slope of her breast and flicking her nipple, his breath warm and moist, as he whispered, "How does this feel?" She shook her head, trying to dislodge the memories, but they returned, stronger and more vivid.

"Show her your arms." Lionel pointed toward Michelle.

Michelle instinctively tugged down on her shirtsleeves.

In the archives of recent memory, Geraldine felt

Elliot's fingers move inside her, first fast, then slow, the pleasure building to a crescendo.

"She needs to see." Lionel waved toward his wife. "She needs to know."

Slowly, Michelle rolled up the sleeve of one arm.

An inky purple bruise bloomed on her dark skin. The mottled color spread like angry fingers on her upper arm.

The memory tape stopped, and Geraldine jolted into the present moment. "Oh, sugar." She gasped, covering her mouth. "What happened?"

"Her boyfriend beat her." Lionel heaved his chest. "Hope wants her to file a domestic violence report with the tribal police. I agree, but I think she should file after she moves here."

Stepping forward, Geraldine opened her arms. "Oh, sugar, of course, you can stay."

Michelle gulped, taking a step backward. "Thank you."

Folding her into an embrace, Geraldine smoothed her hands against Michelle's back. Stark fear and bewildered gratitude radiated like heat from Michelle's skin. Breathing in the dark fragrance of Michelle's hair, she closed her eyes, blocking out the images of violence she imagined the girl must have endured. "Oh, sugar, why didn't you tell us sooner?"

"I was scared." Michelle wriggled out of the hug. "I didn't think you liked me."

For a long moment, Geraldine held Michelle's gaze. If Geraldine had known about the abuse, she would not have judged Lionel so harshly. She would have understood. She wouldn't have hardened her heart and turned away, letting jealousy and possessiveness grip her thoughts and turn her attentions toward the flattery of a strange man whose memory haunted her with both unexpected flashes of supreme delight and bouts of dark remorse. "I'm so sorry. If I had known, I wouldn't have been unkind."

"Apology accepted." Nodding, Michelle glanced at Lionel. "Thank you for your generosity. I'll move my stuff this week."

"Take your time." Lionel touched her shoulder. "You don't want to arouse his suspicion." Glancing from one woman to the other, he removed his cell phone from his pocket. "Now, if you don't mind, I need to call Cassidy to see how quickly he can build a new office." He strode away, the phone nestled against his ear.

Michelle pointed toward the warehouse. "I'll wait for today's shipment."

Alone, Geraldine clasped her hand over her heart to still the ache that grew. Oh, why didn't she ask Lionel more questions about Michelle's situation? She could have intervened in a healthy way, instead of turning her attention toward another man. Dropping her hand from her chest, she stared at the floor. A thought prickled her scalp. How would she react the next time Elliot came into the store? Would she trigger suspicion in her husband? Or could she hide the secret she never wanted to have? Coldness doused her body, and she sank onto the stool beside the meat slicer. What if Elliot showed up and initiated a lover's quarrel in the deli line? Lionel would discover the truth without a confession. Burying her face in her hands, she breathed in the scent of dread that reeked from her pores. Oh, how would she get herself out of this mess?

****

At dinner with Hope and Nick in their mansion on Wapi Mountain, Geraldine nudged the crisp green beans back and forth across her plate and sipped the tangy wine. She recalled the Irish stew she had with Elliot last night, the memory of his hand sliding up her thigh, and how wet she was before he touched her panties.

Hope leaned against the table, her gaze directed at Lionel. "I don't think Michelle should move into the store. She should stay on the reservation and file the domestic violence report. You aren't equipped to deal with these issues." Turning, she pleaded. "Right, Geraldine?"

Thrust from her thoughts, Geraldine set aside her fork and drained the rest of her wine. Flushed from the memories and the alcohol, she staggered to catch the gist of the conversation. "Well...I don't know."

"Hope's right." Nick waved his glass of wine. "First, the property is zoned commercial. Second, the permits will take at least two weeks to get from the city. Third—"

Lionel shook his head. "You never should have disbanded your father's real estate development company. People like me could come to you for help in these circumstances."

Nick slammed his wine glass against the table. A muscle twitched in his jaw. "My father screwed over more than half of Vine Valley, not to mention what he did to the Wapi Indians."

Hope covered his hand with hers. "Honey, not now, please."

"Why not expose the truth?" Nick flashed. "My

father was the wealthiest man in the valley because he owned a portion of everything from everyone." He ran his fingers through his hair. "I spent the last half dozen years undoing as much of the damage as I could, starting with dismantling his crooked corporation."

Rattled by the sudden outburst, Geraldine clutched the napkin in her lap. When her father died, she and Lionel had problems refinancing the store because Nick's father owned the note with a huge prepayment penalty. If Nick hadn't persuaded his father to renegotiate the terms, Geraldine and Lionel would have lost the store. "I don't think Lionel meant what he said. We both know how poorly your father treated others in business."

Nodding, Lionel clenched his fist on the table. "What I was trying to say was I need help. If you still had connections in real estate, you might be able to help me." He uncurled his fist. "You're good at helping others."

Nick shoved back his chair and stood. "Anyone want more wine?"

Staring at her empty glass, Geraldine nodded.

Nick stepped out of the dining room and returned with a fresh bottle, refilling Geraldine's glass.

Lionel stabbed his fork into the veal cordon bleu and sliced off a piece with his knife. "Do we have enough guys to play in the tournament without me? With all that's happening at the moment, I don't want to go."

A leap of panic jolted her attention. The trip to Las Vegas was their one consistent getaway each year. If they didn't go, what would they do? Geraldine placed a hand on his shoulder. "Oh, sugar, let Jeffrey handle the store."

Grumbling, Lionel shook his head. "I just don't feel right leaving Michelle alone."

Dropping her hand, Geraldine steeled her back against the chair. That woman was more important than softball, more important than a romantic getaway with his wife, and more important than the survival of his marriage. Grabbing her glass, she sipped the sharp wine to stop an avalanche of words from tumbling from her mouth.

Lionel speared a few green beans. "You guys go and have fun."

"We'll see if we have enough teammates." Nick scooped a mouthful of wild rice.

Hope motioned toward Geraldine. "Are we getting together for cocktails Thursday night?"

Holding her breath, Geraldine listened to her accelerating heartbeat. She could not risk entering Jasper's and seeing Elliot behind the counter. What if he hinted at their intimacy? Or suggested another get-together? What would she say, especially in front of her friends? The muscles squeezed across her shoulders and down her arms, tensing her fingers against the fork that hovered above the green beans. "Not this week. I'm too busy."

"I understand." Hope sipped from her glass of wine. "You both sound overwhelmed by circumstances. We'll meet up the following week."

A flash of panic swooped through her body. Geraldine dropped her fork. The tines clicked against the china. "You and Deb can go without me. I might have to skip a couple of weeks. Schools are starting, and a lot of our employees will be cutting back to part-time. Lionel and I will be working more hours." She clutched her hands in her lap, wondering how long she could delay the inevitable meeting at Jasper's. "I'll be right back." Standing, she excused herself from the table. Wandering through the hallways, she found the French doors opening to the deck. She stepped outside and gulped the fresh air to steel her nerves. The sky was bruised. A light breeze wafted over her arms, and a crop of goose bumps prickled her skin. Hugging herself, she stared at the starry sky, wondering how long she could live with this dark secret she didn't want to keep.

"What are you doing here, all alone?"

She spun, glimpsing Nick's quick jaunt across the deck to join her at the railing. A weak smile played at the edges of her lips. She had always liked Nick. In high school, she didn't believe he was a ladies' man because of his good looks, just as he didn't believe she lacked intelligence because of her natural beauty. Because of their deeply troubled relationships with their respective fathers, they bonded like siblings over their shared misery. As the years passed, their connection strengthened. She could trust Nick with anything and everything. "I'm thinking."

"Dark thoughts." He arched an eyebrow.

The way he said the phrase—flat without an inflection at the end—made it sound decisive, like he knew. "Bad thoughts." She clasped her hands and leaned against the railing, listening to the crickets and the frogs sing off-key.

"Disturbing thoughts." He matched her body language.

"Damning thoughts." She heaved a sigh. A chill wind whisked her arms, and she shuddered. She didn't want to return to the dinner party.

"We can't run away from ourselves."

When he spoke, he sounded like a disembodied voice, his silhouette barely noticeable in the remaining light.

"We also can't hide forever."

She waved a hand, dismissing his statements. "Oh, sugar, I just don't want to be my father."

He nodded. "And I don't want to be mine."

She leaned away from the railing, rubbing her hands up and down her chilled arms.

"Let's go inside." He gestured toward the light through the French doors.

Shaking her head, she tilted away her body. "I can't face the others."

"You can't face yourself."

Gasping, she widened her eyes. "How much do you know?"

He cocked his head to the side and grinned. "How much do you want to tell me?"

She laughed. "Your wife might have taught you some of her divinatory skills."

"Hardly." He chuckled. "I just know you too well." He wrapped an arm around her shoulders and steered her toward the stairs. "Let's walk to keep you warm."

Leaning against him, she sank into the comfort of his presence. He had been through a lot, too, having a father whose morals conflicted with his own. If she told him, he would keep her secret, he would give good advice, and he would help her in a way no one else could. Step by step, she matched Nick's stride down the stairs and across the meadow toward the twinkling lights of the gazebo against the velvet sky. "I've been unfaithful." She gulped. "I hate myself for what I've done."

He dipped his head and squeezed her shoulder. "Is the affair over?"

She snickered. "I wouldn't call it an affair, but more of a one-time mistake."

"Does the man know it's over?"

Nodding, she snuggled closer. "I told him we can't even be friends."

"Good for you." He rubbed her upper arm with his warm hand. "Want to take a seat or keep walking?"

The lit gazebo seemed like a stage. "Let's keep walking."

He continued with his slow stride. "And Lionel doesn't know, and you don't want to tell him, right?"

"Right." She flashed a sidelong glance. "Does that make me a bad person?"

A muscle in his jaw twitched. "When I dismantled my father's real estate development company after he died, I was so determined to right the perceived wrongs I had witnessed growing up that I neglected to consider the big picture—how the company employed hundreds of people with families. I just focused on what I thought was the problem. Only later, after witnessing the aftermath of my self-righteous decision, did I realize the real estate development company was not the problem. How my father used the company for his own malicious purpose was."

He stopped and met her gaze. "Your father wasn't a bad man. He made some poor decisions by taking sexual advantage of some of his employees, hiding the fact from your mother, and entrusting you with his secret. But he also built the first grocery store in Vine

Valley with a comprehensive program to feed the poor through donating salvageable goods, instead of tossing them into the dumpster like other businesses would. And he helped make you—wonderful, beautiful you." He braced his hands on her shoulders. "You need to forgive your dad, so you can forgive yourself. I'm not saying it's easy. I've forgiven my father, but I still get angry sometimes as you saw tonight."

Blinking, she shook her head. "What if Lionel finds out and he wants to divorce me? Where will I go? What will I do? He's everything to me."

"Is he?" Nick dropped his hands. "Or are you just too comfortable to leave? Maybe that's why you cheated. You wanted a quick excuse to end things."

Tipping back her head, she searched the stars. "I cheated because I had the opportunity to cheat. We were alone, at his house, and he kissed me as an invitation to more." She met Nick's gaze. "I stopped short of intercourse, but the damage was already done by then." She pivoted back toward the house. "I was angry with Lionel. He's been obsessed with helping Michelle. Their relationship has triggered the grief he had over the loss of our twins, and he blamed me for their deaths." She shuddered. "He apologized this morning. But it was too little, too late. I had already fooled around with another man."

Nick walked her back toward the house, his stride matching hers. "After my big mistake with the real estate development company, I evaluated each asset separately for both the pros and the cons before making a decision about what to do. The process helped tremendously." He paused. "What's the good in your marriage? What's the bad? Where do you want to go with what you have?"

Good questions, good advice.

Moving ahead, he climbed the stairs to the deck and opened the French doors.

She stepped inside the envelope of warmth and listened to the banter from the dining room as Lionel and Hope talked. Following Nick, she wound her way back toward the room.

Lionel waved. "Hey, GG, Hope was telling me a story about Beaver Dam. Have you heard it before?"

Pulling back the chair beside him, she shook her head. "No, I haven't." As she settled in to listen to Hope's story, she couldn't avoid Nick's questions echoing in her mind. What was good about her marriage? What was bad? And, most importantly, where did she want to go from here?

Chapter Seventeen

Time. Lionel needed more time, which he did not have.

Two weeks for a building permit…

Another three weeks to construct a new office…

Already Michelle went to her second visit with the OB/GYN. She had started the first week of her second trimester. Soon she would start to show, and then Paul would know she did not have that abortion.

Listening to Cassidy and his crew as they surveyed the space of the warehouse, Lionel scratched the back of his neck.

"What if we modify the existing configuration?" Cassidy pointed to a maintenance closet filled with brooms, mops, and vacuums. "I don't need a remodel permit to install an air-conditioning vent in a closet."

Lionel crossed both arms over his chest. "Is it big enough?"

With a tape, Cassidy measured the dimensions. "The desk and a chair will fit, but not much else." He placed his hands on his hips and tossed back his sandy hair. "Sound like a plan?"

Lionel mulled over the suggestion. Should he ask his wife? With a sidelong glance through the plastic curtain, he glimpsed her gesturing to a customer in the deli line. Sinews tightened across his shoulders. Did he dare brave the rush of her unpredictable hormones without sparking another fight? Turning toward Cassidy, he waved. "Go ahead."

"Great. I'll send Derrick to buy the supplies, and Shawn will help with the installation." Cassidy wrote in his notebook.

"How long will it take?" Lionel furrowed his brow.

Shrugging, Cassidy tapped the notebook with his pencil. "One or two days. We'll be finished before the weekend."

"Perfect." Lionel heaved a sigh of relief. Michelle could tell that no-good boyfriend goodbye on Friday. He rubbed his forehead. Now if only he could convince his wife to get some help for her moods…more for his sake than for hers. He clapped Cassidy's shoulder. "Hey, do you mind if I ask a personal question?"

Glancing from side to side, Cassidy frowned. "There's not a lot of privacy."

Lionel led him through the door to the outside. The exhaust of cars leaving the parking lot mingled with the sweet scent of wild grass. Squinting from the afternoon sunlight, he strode over to the field and stood beneath a tree. The air was dry and mild. A rustle of birds in the branches sounded like people whispering.

"What's going on?" Cassidy folded his arms across his chest and broadened his stance.

"Geraldine's been acting funny lately. Not quite herself. I'm just wondering if maybe you have some experience with Deb going through the change of life."

Shaking his head, Cassidy whistled soft and low. "Deb's not anywhere near that stage. She's still struggling with the romantic factor." He chuckled. "Last week, she dressed up in sexy lingerie. She appeared so awkward and uncomfortable I found her

147

adorable." With the toe of his shoe, he kicked at a crisp leaf in the dirt. "I don't know what to tell you about Geraldine. Is she moody? Withdrawn?"

"All of the above." Lionel raised his gaze toward the sky and studied the clouds through the sparse branches. He couldn't remember when her last period was or any of that technical information that doctors ask. She had been tearful a couple of nights ago and angry and withdrawn during the following days. Whenever he approached her, he braced himself for an onslaught of powerful emotions that didn't correspond to whatever they were discussing. "She's irrational and angry, and her outbursts scare me."

Frowning, Cassidy crossed his arms over his chest. "Is something else going on? Something not related to her cycle?"

Lionel breathed in deeply and sighed. "Oh, course, you're right. This whole business with Michelle has gotten her crazy." He scratched the back of his neck. "No matter what I say, Geraldine thinks I'm stepping out of bounds by helping too much. She thinks I should mind my own business."

"Really?" Cassidy laughed and threw open his arms. "Mrs. I'm-Saving-the-Universe-One-Sandwich-at-a-Time accused you of not minding your own business?"

A crooked smile creased Lionel's face. "That's right. She's fine when she's meddling, but she's upset when I'm meddling."

Cassidy patted Lionel's shoulder. "You go set her straight."

"How?" Lionel lifted his eyebrows. Doubt clouded his chest.

"Get her involved. Make it her problem." Cassidy pointed toward the store. "Ask her how she wants to decorate Michelle's room." He smiled. "Every woman likes to transform a space into a home."

Thinking, Lionel nodded. He remembered Cassidy's ex-wife, Stephanie, decorating their home after his parents died. She boxed the knickknacks and family heirlooms and replaced them with items she bought from flea markets and discount stores—throw pillows, framed prints, scented candles, and area rugs. The idea sounded good, and he flushed with hope. He clapped Cassidy's shoulder. "You better be right, because I don't think I can tolerate much more of her nonsense."

****

After her shift at the deli ended, Geraldine drove to see Deb. With the windows rolled down, she steered through the suburban streets with a sad love song playing on the satellite radio. The brunt of summer had finally shifted, with the heat mellowing to a caress on her bare arm and the cool wind whipping the hair away from her face. The singer's voice warbled about love gone wrong, and Geraldine snapped off the stereo, driving in silence until she pulled up to the ranch-style home and parked. Stepping out into the late afternoon sunlight, she slung her purse over one shoulder and shielded her eyes with her other hand.

Deb waved from where she sat on the porch swing, an open book in her lap.

Beneath the shade of the apple tree, Adam sat on his heels, pulling handfuls of grass. He was tall, almost as tall as Cassidy, and lanky with the same mop of curls his father had. Tilting his face toward the sky, he tossed the errant grass into the air and giggled as the blades fell like confetti against his shoulders.

Geraldine glimpsed Adam. A pang of pity squeezed her chest. How did Cassidy, and now Deb, endure the disappointment of having an adult disabled child? She unlocked the gate and stepped into the front yard. "Hi, Adam!" She plunged a hand into her purse and withdrew a ham and cheese sandwich. "Want a snack?"

Standing on his gazelle-like legs, Adam shuffled. When he was within reach, he lunged for the sandwich.

Laughing, Geraldine raised her arm until the sandwich was just out of reach. "Let's go inside and wash those hands first."

Deb linked her arm through Adam's and steered him toward the house. "Follow Aunty Geraldine."

Inside the stuffy kitchen, Deb helped Adam soap and rinse his hands.

As usual, Geraldine grabbed a plate from the cupboard and a knife from the drawer and sliced the sandwich into bite-sized strips. She sat next to Adam and handed him one piece at a time.

With the palm of a hand, he shoved the bits of sandwich into his mouth, chewed, and swallowed. Extending his arm, he wiggled his fingers. "More, please."

Smiling, Geraldine handed him another piece.

Deb placed three glasses of iced water on the table and took the other seat next to Adam. "How've you been? We missed you on Thursday."

The true reason for her absence lodged beneath her ribs. "Busy, sugar. Lionel and I hired three part-time employees. Training is always a hassle." She glanced at

Deb before returning her gaze to Adam who was munching. She didn't want to talk about anything serious around him. "How are you doing?"

"I'm fine."

Glancing at the near-empty plate, Geraldine handed Adam the last piece of ham and cheese on sourdough. "I do have some gossip. We're remodeling the store for Michelle to move in this weekend. She's leaving her boyfriend and having a baby. Can you imagine being eighteen, unmarried, and pregnant?"

"No, I can't." Deb laughed, helping Adam wash his hands at the sink again. "I can barely believe I'm a stepmom to an adult." She kissed Adam on the cheek. "You want to go back outside or listen to music in your room?"

Adam widened his smile. "Music."

Deb pointed toward the hall. "I'll set up his music and come back so we can visit some more." She touched Geraldine's shoulder.

Alone, in the kitchen, Geraldine rinsed the plate and knife and placed them in the dishwasher. Returning to the table, she sank into the chair and gripped the cold sides of the glass of iced water. Just a few nights ago, in Elliot's apartment, she sat at his small, round kitchen table, waiting for dinner to be served, unaware of any further implications. She shivered from the memory of his hands on her arms, his breath on her neck, and his tongue running a line between her breasts. The creak of the floorboards in the hallway startled her out of her reverie, and she gasped, lifting her head.

"Are you sure you're all right?" Frowning, Deb took the seat beside her.

"Fine, sugar." She took a sip of the stark water, all

of her senses suddenly awake and alive. "What were you reading out there?"

"Oh, the book." Deb stood and wandered outside, returning with the paperback. "This is the proof copy of Cassidy's first book of poems." Smiling, she held out the copy. "I convinced him to self-publish."

Nature by Cassidy Burke featured a blue jay perched on a bare branch. Turning the glossy cover in her hands, Geraldine flipped through the pages of type. "I'm sure it's wonderful. I'm just not much into reading." She placed the book on the table. "But Lionel will ask me to buy a few copies as Christmas presents for all the staff, so I should probably place my order now."

"Cassidy will be thrilled." Deb tucked the book beside her, stroking the glossy cover with her fingertips. "I'm so proud of him."

The radiant happiness emanating from her smile blindsided Geraldine. When was the last time she was proud of Lionel? "I'm glad for you, sugar." Geraldine patted her friend's wrist.

Deb tilted her head to the side. "Something's wrong. I sense it."

"Oh, no." Geraldine groaned. "Not you, too."

"What do you mean?" Wrinkling her forehead, Deb scooted closer. "Who else knows?"

Not wanting to be the center of gossip, Geraldine flicked her wrist. "Let's talk about something else, please."

"No, let's not." Deb frowned. "I'm worried about you. Please, tell me."

Backed into a corner, Geraldine sighed. "Oh, Nick was just talking the other day about my need to forgive my father."

"Didn't you do that already?" Deb glanced at the ceiling and counted on her fingers. "Was it eight or nine years ago?"

"Eight and a half, to be exact." Geraldine sipped the iced water. "Nick Senior was still alive. Remember how I had to negotiate with him? He wouldn't let me assume the loan."

"What a pain that man was." Deb shook her head. "I don't care how much he donated to the church." She narrowed her gaze. "But why would Nick mention all of that old stuff, especially during a social situation?"

Geraldine rubbed her damp hands against her cheeks. "Because we were talking, and I mentioned how I don't want to become my father."

Tossing back her head, Deb laughed. "You're *nothing* like him."

The pressure mounted in Geraldine's chest. "I *am* my father."

Adam wandered into the kitchen, holding out his tablet. "Song."

"Hold that thought, Geraldine." Deb grasped the tablet and scrolled through the listings. "Do you want to listen to this song?" After a glance at Adam, she tapped on a picture on the screen. Electric guitars and drums blasted from the speakers.

"Thank you." Adam snatched the tablet and hugged it to his chest. Turning, he left the room.

"Where were we?" Deb stood and refilled their glasses with water. "Oh, yes, forgiving your father…and how you're nothing like him. But now you say you are." She shook her head. "Nothing you're saying makes sense unless you're not telling me something."

Swallowing another gulp of iced water, Geraldine bowed her head, unable to form the words she wanted to say. Tightness constricted her throat. Deb was right. She wasn't exactly like her father, taking sexual advantage of employees, but she wasn't exactly innocent either. "I...flirted...a little...too far."

"Too far?" Deb widened her eyes. "Do you mean you cheated on Lionel?"

A small nod issued from Geraldine's chin. She clasped her hands over her face and sobbed. "I don't know how I let it happen, but I did. And now I don't know what to do." She hiccupped. "I'm so sorry."

Reaching over, Deb touched Geraldine's shoulder. "Well...let's start at the beginning."

After wiping her eyes with the back of her hand, Geraldine grabbed the glass of water and took four long swallows. Thinking back to the moment she first understood the attraction between her and Elliot, she shrugged. "He was a few years younger, and he treated me like I was a few years younger, too." Heat burned her face. "I flirted, and he flirted back. Then he came to the deli and ordered a sandwich and invited me to dinner. Since my plans with Hope and Nick had been canceled because Lionel closed for another employee, I was alone for the night."

She inhaled deeply, wondering if she should have declined the invitation. Then she wouldn't be here confessing to her best friend about her unexpected sexual encounter with a man she never wanted to see again. She picked up the glass and studied the water wobbling on the inside surface. "I went to his house for dinner, and one thing led to another." She met her friend's curious gaze. "It happened so fast." She set the glass on the table. "I don't know if it's any consolation, but I stopped short of intercourse." She dipped her head, more tears pricking her eyes.

"Oh, my, Geraldine, I don't know what to tell you." Deb gasped. "When I fell for Cassidy, I was a nun, so technically, I cheated, too. I was married to God, and I broke my vows, but I asked for forgiveness, and I was forgiven." She frowned. "Have you told Lionel?"

Keeping secrets from her husband wasn't something she did. She couldn't even hide a birthday present. But this transgression lodged deep in her body like an extra bone, and she carried its weight with awkwardness. She shook her head. "You and Nick are the only ones I've told."

"What about the other man?" Deb flattened her hands on the table. "Does he know you're married?"

"He knows everything." Geraldine groaned. "I never want to see him again."

"Then don't."

Geraldine squeezed her hands together. She couldn't keep his identity a secret and avoid a future encounter, could she? "I need you to do me a favor and tell Hope we need to find a new meeting spot for our girls' night out."

"Why do we—?" Deb slapped her forehead and gasped. "Oh, no, the guy was Elliot."

Biting her lower lip, Geraldine nodded. Heat raced across her cheeks. "I don't want everyone to know."

"Then you shouldn't have chosen Elliot." Deb narrowed her gaze. "He's not from here. He doesn't know your history. He doesn't care about your reputation."

"He's a businessman." Geraldine remembered the softness in his eyes when he asked if they could be friends. Oh, how horrible she felt to say no, but she couldn't risk the temptation of being around him again. "He understands professionalism."

"He also does business with Nick, attends our senior softball games, and volunteers at the church." Deb threw up her arms. "He's a big deal in the community. You can't avoid him forever."

Cringing, Geraldine blocked the thoughts from her mind. "I just want to keep this whole thing a secret."

"But it's not just your secret to keep. It's also his."

Fear prickled her scalp, and Geraldine closed her eyes. She never imagined Elliot bragging to others about their brief liaison. But Deb was right. He could tell anyone anything about what had happened, and she was powerless to stop him. Groaning, she clutched her hair in her hands. Oh, why had she let him touch her all over? Now she had to endure the aftermath of deceit and self-loathing while hoping the other man kept his mouth shut.

Groaning, Deb shook her head. "Why did you choose Elliot?"

"I didn't choose him." Geraldine flashed a sidelong glance. "He chose me."

"Explain." Deb pursed her lips together.

"He came into the deli and called me 'pretty lady'." Geraldine dabbed at the corners of her eyes. "He made me feel special again." She gulped. "Ever since I stopped having sex with Lionel, I haven't felt special. His paying attention to Michelle was the proverbial straw that broke the camel's back." Clutching a fist to her mouth, she stifled a sob.

Deb touched her shoulder. "Of course, Elliot made you feel special. He's a bigger flirt than you are."

Nodding, Geraldine tugged her lips into a straight line. "Yes, he is. I was jealous of the attention he paid you at Jasper's the first time we went."

"Jealous? Of me?" Raising her eyebrows, Deb tapped her chest with her fingertips. "I'm hardly as beautiful as you are."

Geraldine chuckled. "You're sweet. You're innocent. Guys like those qualities in a woman."

Deb flashed a smile. "Cassidy has been intent on corrupting me."

"As all good husbands should." Geraldine winked.

"Lionel is a good husband." A dark cloud passed over Deb's face. "He can't help the way his body is aging. Don't take his inability to perform in the bedroom personally, or you'll end up as miserable as I am trying to be the type of seductress I think Cassidy needs."

"You're right. I haven't been kind." Geraldine grumbled. "Nick even suggested I cheated as an easy way out of the marriage."

Widening her eyes, Deb gasped. "Why would you leave a good man for a flirt?"

Biting her lower lip, Geraldine leaned her back against the chair. "I don't like to think about my marriage or examine it too closely. I'm scared of what I will find out."

Deb leaned forward and crossed her hands on the table. "Tell me more. You need to discover whether or not you want to stay or go."

"You sound like Nick." Shaking her head,

Geraldine curled a hand into a loose fist. "Nick asked me to list the good and the bad in the marriage. I can't even come up with five things."

"Lionel and you share a history." Deb raised one finger. "You share a business and a home and a dog." She lifted three more fingers. "You love each other." She flattened her palm, spreading her fingers wide. "Five reasons."

"The bad list feels longer." Geraldine uncurled her fingers. "Lionel's loyal to Michelle. He can't make love anymore without help, and he doesn't want help." She dropped her hand and flashed a crooked smile. "But he tries. He's romantic in his own way. He can't cook, but he dresses up the table like it is Thanksgiving when he serves takeout. Whenever we go to Vegas for a softball tournament, he splurges on the best hotel room." She propped an elbow on the table and cupped her chin in her hand. "He leaves me a half pot of coffee before he goes to work."

Deb nodded. "All valid reasons to stick together and work out things." After picking up her glass of water, she took a sip. "But believe me, the road ahead is hard. You'll have to come clean and rebuild trust and hold each other accountable. Can you do it?"

Geraldine shrugged. "I don't know."

"Well, at least you're honest." Deb patted her shoulder. "During my confession, Father Anthony told me once you stop thinking of 'we' and start thinking of 'me,' the relationship is over. That's how I ended up having the affair with Cassidy. I stopped thinking of my commitment to God and started thinking of my selfish needs to be in a relationship with someone I could see and touch and talk to who could see and touch and talk with me. I broke my vows to pursue what I craved."

Geraldine lifted her eyebrows. "Any regrets?"

Sighing, Deb cupped the glass of water with both hands. "Sometimes I believe it is easier to love someone perfect like God than to love someone flawed like Cassidy." She tapped her fingers against the side of the glass. "No decision is perfect. You have to make up your mind with what little you know and trust the outcome will be better than you imagined." Standing, she hugged her friend. "Good luck. I'll be praying for you."

"Thanks, sugar." Geraldine patted her back, breathing in deeply the scent of her friend's flowery shampoo. "I promise to consider everything you've said." A swell of appreciation filled her chest, even as the dread of deciding what to do rested like a weighted blanket on her shoulders.

Chapter Eighteen

After leaving Deb's house, Geraldine decided to drive downtown to talk to Elliot one last time. She arrived at the cusp of happy hour. A gaggle of women flocked around the bar, leaning on their crossed arms, and shoving cleavage toward Elliot who snuck glances between filling drink orders.

She clenched the strap of her purse, her heart knocking against her ribs. Why was she here? What did she hope to accomplish? Hadn't she said everything that needed to be said the other night?

Deb's words floated through her mind. *It's not just your secret to keep. It's also his.*

Pushing back her shoulders, she took a wobbly step toward the bar. She needed reassurance Elliot would not speak of their encounter to anyone. She could not afford to lose the rest of what she had—her husband, her reputation, her dignity—after she had already lost her fidelity and self-respect. Slipping onto an empty bar stool, she clutched her purse in her lap and waited.

Elliot pivoted, glancing down the bar. When their gazes met, he drew his eyebrows together. After pulling away from the counter, he tucked a tip into the glass jar beside the register before picking up a dish towel and wiping his hands. "What brings you here?"

At least, he hadn't called her pretty lady. She swallowed, regaining her voice. "I'd like to talk with you, if you have a moment."

He stared into her eyes and nodded. Lifting a hand, he waved across the restaurant to an employee. "Stuart, do you mind covering for ten?" As soon as he was relieved, Elliot slipped out from behind the bar and waved her toward the back door.

She didn't want to be seen, but she also didn't want to be alone with him. The temptation might spark another unwanted encounter. Shaking her head, she pointed toward the street. "Let's walk." If she stood far enough away, no one would suspect the topic of their conversation.

He strode toward the front door, holding it open.

A gust of cool air swept over her arms, and she shivered. A bank of fog hovered near the horizon just below the rays of the sun. Cars traveled bumper-to-bumper along the main street. Tourists littered the sidewalk, ducking into boutique shops or stopping to take pictures at the clock tower in Courthouse Square. The smells of exhaust and perfume clotted the air. Geraldine dodged the crowds, careful to keep a shoulder width of space between her and Elliot.

Shoving his hands into his pockets, he squinted at the sunlight. "I thought you were clear the other night about not being my friend or my lover." He matched her stride. "What do you want to talk about?"

She gave him a sidelong glance. "Please, promise you won't tell anyone what happened between us."

"Is that all you're worried about?" He lifted his eyebrows. "Who would I possibly tell?"

On her fingers, she counted. "My husband, the players on the Vine Valley Crushers, the parishioners at your church, my employees, your employees, and anyone else either of us knows."

He chuckled. "Seriously, you think I know that many people?"

She shrugged. "I don't really know you. You could be vindictive or malicious."

Frowning, he paused beneath the awning of a storefront window. "I'm none of those things. Are you?"

"No, I'm not." A prickly sensation spread throughout her body. He didn't know her, either. They were both fantasies—figments of their imaginations acted upon without the awareness of consequences. Through her, he had imagined the perfect friend and lover, playful and noncommittal. Through him, she had envisioned the perfect flirtation, someone who did not know her history and would not judge her. Neither had believed reality mattered until the fantasy no longer existed.

She rubbed the goose bumps on her arms and lifted her chin. At her core, she was a middle-aged woman, a long-term wife, and a second-generation business owner. The rest of her identity wavered in the periphery, ready to be tested. When she crossed the threshold of fantasy to reality by allowing their flirtation to manifest into something more, she had discovered she was as fallible as her father, whom she had punished with her judgment. Even if Lionel never knew about her indiscretion, she knew. She was subjected to her court of opinion and a prisoner to her mistake forever, unless she chose to release herself with the gift of absolution.

In talking to Elliot about her need for his silence, she was confirming his complicity and acknowledging her guilt. Talking would not reclaim that part of her she had momentarily relinquished. Nothing would. So, why was she here? She tightened her arms around her waist to brace against a gust of wind and her worries. She gazed off into the distance between the fog bank and the sunshine. "I'm sorry about the other night. I shouldn't have accepted your dinner invitation. I should have drawn the line at our friendly banter." Sighing, she met his gaze.

He smiled, and the lines crinkled around his green eyes. "No apology needed."

Turning, she strode in the direction of the bar and grill. An unexpected release emanated down her legs, lightening her step.

He stopped beside the doors of the bar and removed his hands from his pockets. "Don't worry. I won't tell anyone."

"Thank you." From her purse, her cell phone pinged. She stepped aside and unzipped the main compartment. Swiping her finger across the screen, she read the message from Lionel.

—*Are you still at the mattress store? I just got home. Has Noelle been fed?*—

She raised a hand to her mouth. In her preoccupation and haste, she had forgotten Lionel had asked her to purchase a mattress for Michelle on her way home from work. She glanced at the time. Six o'clock. Was the mattress store still open?

Elliot peered over her shoulder. "Is something wrong?"

Shaking her head, she clutched the phone against her chest.

Elliot pursed his lips. "He doesn't know you're

here, does he?"

The darkness in his green eyes captured the doubt deep in her bones.

"Maybe you should tell him." He yanked back the door. "I have to get back to work. If you and your girlfriends decide to patronize another bar, I understand. Goodnight."

"Goodbye, Elliot." She waited for the door to close before she lowered her hand and typed.

—*Haven't fed Noelle. At mattress store. Be home soon.*—

****

Fifteen minutes lapsed into an hour. Tired of waiting, Lionel grabbed a beer from the nearly empty refrigerator and strode into the living room. He flipped on the TV to distract himself from the growing emptiness in his stomach and settled into the recliner, sipping the ice-cold bitterness that warmed his insides. If he had known Geraldine's response to his text message meant she would be home an hour or two later, he would have driven to the nearest fast-food restaurant and bought dinner.

Noelle limped into the room and curled at the foot of the recliner, her head nestled between her paws.

Lionel bent down and stroked the fur along her back. A low rumble of snores rattled beneath his hand, and he grabbed the remote to flip through the channels, searching for something to occupy his interest other than his dark thoughts. Images and sound danced from the screen, filling the room with color and movement. The joints in his lower back ached, and he shifted against the worn cushions, searching for a comfortable spot. Sipping the beer, he relaxed as the liquid comfort wound through his muscles. He settled on a sitcom, hoping the fictional people with their imaginary problems would propel him out of his misery.

Minutes later, the garage door powered up, and the *clip-clop* of Geraldine's heels clattered across the kitchen. Glancing at the clock against the wall, he frowned. Seven-fifteen.

"Hey, sugar." Geraldine leaned against the doorway, her arms crossed over her chest. "The double bed I bought for Michelle will be delivered tomorrow. I stopped by Southern Kitchen and picked up some fried chicken and mashed potatoes for dinner. Are you hungry?"

"I've been hungry since I texted you." He frowned. "What took you so long? You left work at four-thirty."

"I stopped by Deb's house to chat." She pointed toward the dining room. "Let's eat."

He switched off the TV and stood, arching his back. Walking around the sleeping dog, he followed his wife. Taking his seat at the head of the table, he folded his hands and waited.

She unpacked the bags and set the table. She selected the breast and wings, his favorite parts, and ladled gravy on mounds of mashed potatoes. "*Bon appétit.*" She piled her plate full and sat beside him.

Biting into the crispy, greasy chicken breast, he closed his eyes and savored the spicy flavor of the company's signature Cajun recipe.

"How was your day?" She sipped from the plastic straw in her soda.

"Fine. Cassidy finished the closet-to-office conversion, and his crew moved the computer, desk, and chair into the room." He finished the rest of his beer and stood to get another. When he returned, he took a long sip. "Thanks for getting the mattress."

"You're welcome." She ran her fingers along the length of her cup. "I also bought two sets of sheets."

He frowned, studying her gestures. She was nervous. He stiffened, worried about what she was thinking, wondering if it had anything to do with why she was so late coming home. "You okay?"

Nodding, she flicked her glance around the room.

"How was your visit with Deb?" He searched her face.

She leaned back against the chair and wiped her hands on a napkin. "She's so happy. Cassidy's self-publishing a book of poems."

"Romeo finally made his threat come true." He chuckled. "We'll have to buy copies for our staff."

She smiled. "I already placed our order, sugar."

The mashed potatoes and gravy tasted smooth and salty. He washed it down with another sip of bitter beer. "Was the mattress store busy?"

"Not really. I was their last customer."

"Was Southern Kitchen packed?"

She shrugged. "Not more than usual. Why?"

The amount of time it took to run to the mattress store and visit with Deb did not account for the time she was gone. After all, she didn't particularly care for furniture shopping, and Deb was always preoccupied with Adam, having to stick to a strict routine. When he considered her jittery movements and her hesitancy to elaborate on the conversation, he felt a knot tighten in his stomach. He was sure she was hiding something. "Stop anywhere else?" He narrowed his gaze.

Stroking the sides of the cup, she stared at her plate

of untouched food. "I went by Jasper's and had a conversation with Elliot."

"Why?" Frowning, he gnawed the last stringy bit of moist meat from a chicken wing.

She fiddled with the straw. "I wanted him to know the girls and I won't be having drinks there on Thursdays."

"Why not?" The hairs at the back of his neck bristled, and he searched her face, willing her to meet his gaze. When she didn't, he moved aside the bones and picked up his beer. The cold liquid slid down his throat, and the knot tightened in his stomach. Something definitely was wrong.

Bowing her head, she stared at the mashed potatoes on her plate. "The last conversation I had with Elliot left me feeling uncomfortable."

He grabbed a napkin and wiped his oily hands. "What did you guys talk about?" Staring at her unreadable expression, he flinched as his insides boiled. "Did he harass you?"

She placed a hand against the table. "We were flirting, as usual, and he asked me to have an affair." She lifted her gaze. "I said no. That's why we can't patronize his restaurant anymore."

"Jesus." He sucked in a breath and tossed the balled-up napkin on the table. The knot unraveled in his stomach. "Does anyone else know?"

She shook her head.

He sensed the story contained more than she was telling, but he didn't know what to ask. Elliot propositioned his wife, and Geraldine said no. So why did he feel like something else was wrong? "You're not telling me everything."

Widening her gaze, she dropped her hand into her lap. "What more is there to say?"

He slapped his thighs and scooted back his chair. Standing, he paced the length of the room. "You know I told you to stay away. He's an opportunist, a ladies' man, and a no-good scoundrel." He pivoted, his body filling the space before her. "Why did you have to walk into his trap, GG?"

"I'm sorry." She bowed her head. "It won't happen again."

"It should not have happened in the first place." He pointed at her chest. "You know better, but for some reason, you can't stop encouraging men with their advances." How many times had he spoken these exact same words? Could he count that high? A montage of memories floated through his mind—GG flirting with the soda delivery guy, GG rollicking in laughter at a teammate's jokes, GG letting her fingers linger too long in a customer's hand as she counted out the change, GG picking up the mail at the post office and winking at the postal clerk, GG dropping off an overdue book at the library and leaning over to expose a bit of cleavage to get out of paying the small fine. How many times did she push the boundary between harmless fun and dangerous liaison? He threw up his arms and shook his fists at the ceiling. "How do I know you aren't to blame?"

She dipped her head and smoothed a hand along the length of her lap. "Are you saying I should have kept this information a secret?"

"No, I'm saying this incident shouldn't have happened." He placed his hands on his hips and broadened his stance. "Elliot isn't the first man you've tempted too far."

Blinking, she raised her head and gaped.

Why was she playing the dumb blonde? He heaved a sigh. "Do I need to remind you of all the other men you've flirted with a little too far? Or do you think I don't know or don't care?" He released his arms and bowed his head. "All my life, I've struggled to be everything for you, and this dance with danger is what I get." Lifting his head, he glowered. "Someday you won't be so lucky, and some guy will take advantage of you. Then what am I to do? Rescue my unfaithful wife from the scoundrel?" He sank into his chair and cradled his head in his hands. "Oh, GG, I know I'm old, and I can't perform like I used to, but I thought you'd stick with me."

"I *am* with you." She scooted closer, touching his shoulder.

He flinched. "You're here because you have no place else to go."

She sighed, dropping her hand to the side. "That's not true."

"Then why do you stay if I'm not enough?" He searched her face. "Why aren't you in Elliot's arms?"

She swallowed and held his gaze. "Because I love you."

Frowning, he studied her face: the lines of confusion in her forehead, the distress cupping the sides of her mouth, and the tension in her jaw. "Love is not enough." He shifted, and the legs of the chair creaked. "What is the real reason?"

Sighing, she dropped her gaze. "You're not the only one who doesn't like growing old." She tugged at the hem on her shirt. "I don't like the wrinkles and the crow's feet and the crepe-paper skin." She blinked. "I'm not as pretty as I was when you met me." She flicked a glance, her eyes moist. "Seeing you fawn all over Michelle and that baby doesn't help, either." Touching her nose with the back of her hand, she stopped a sniffle. "I'm sorry I couldn't give you children. I know you're still not over that fact, and that's part of the reason why you're so invested in Michelle. But I feel neglected. Like you've chosen her over me." She gulped. "That's why I flirted with Elliot. He made me feel alive, like I mattered, like I was someone important, and like I was as good as I used to be when I was as young as Michelle."

Her hard stare barreled down into the pit of his soul. He flinched. Oh, how could they be a continent away from each other with their respective concerns and disappointments? Wasn't a marriage supposed to yoke them together like two oxen standing side by side, sharing the same load? Or was that just another fairy tale? He clasped his hands between his knees and bowed his head, mulling over her words. Yes, she was sensitive about her age and insecure about her failure to provide him with sons and daughters. Yes, he had neglected her over his concerns for Michelle and her unborn baby. But those reasons weren't excuses for her reckless behavior. "I'm worried this thing with Elliot is different. He's a stranger in town. He doesn't know your history like the other guys you flirt with do."

"What are you saying?" A tremor rippled across her lower lip.

Why was she shivering? He wrapped an arm around her and tugged her close until their shoulders touched. The warmth of his body diffused against the ice of her skin. "I'm saying you're more like your father than you think you are. You crave excitement and attention. You need to be wanted sexually, and I can no longer fulfill that need in you. I'm afraid you'll turn to a man like Elliot who can promise you something I can no longer deliver." He tightened his grip. "GG, you mean the world to me. Please, promise me you won't destroy us."

Bowing her head, she sniffled. "I'm sorry."

Why was she sorry unless she was guilty? He stopped rubbing her arm. "How far did he go?"

"What do you mean?" Widening her eyes, she nudged out of his embrace.

"How far did you let him go?" A sour taste bit into his tongue. He held her gaze.

Silence unraveled the truth.

He dropped his hand from her arm. "Is that why you've been moody and withdrawn these past few days? You've been thinking of him and of how far you could take this thing without getting caught like your father with his pants around his ankles in the storeroom, right?" He balled his hands into fists. "And I'm the fool who thought you were starting menopause." He barked with bitter laughter.

Noelle wandered into the dining room.

He patted the dog's head. "Sorry to wake you, ol' girl. Mommy and Daddy are having a talk. That's all."

Geraldine tucked her hands underneath her armpits. "I said I was sorry. I have no intention of ever speaking with Elliot again."

"How can I trust you?" He rubbed Noelle behind the ears. "How do I know you won't slip up and become a cheating bastard like your father who asked you to cover up things so your mother wouldn't find out?" He released Noelle and sank back against the chair, folding his arms over his chest. "How do I know you're telling me the whole truth?" He huffed, remembering her absence at Nick's house. "Why were you gone from the dinner table so long at Nick's house? Were you two making out somewhere?"

Widening her eyes, she touched a hand to her chest and gasped. "Nick and I would never betray you. He's like a brother to me." She narrowed her gaze. "You know that."

"Do I?" He flinched, and a vein throbbed in his forehead. Sure, the two of them palled around since high school. He frowned, remembering how the students voted them the most attractive, even though Nick was dating someone else, and GG was dating him. Suspicion danced across his shoulders. Nick was always so helpful, volunteering to negotiate with his father to eliminate of the prepayment penalty on the store's loan so he and GG could refinance. Maybe Nick's solicitous nature masked something more than brotherly love. He slapped a hand on the table. "Do I need to call Hope and ask her if you're having an affair with her husband?"

"We were talking in the backyard."

"You could have talked at the dining room table."

She threw up her arms. "It was a private conversation."

"Like your conversation with Elliot tonight."

She clutched the sides of her head and groaned. "Do I need to tell you every little thing?"

"Yes, you do."

Taking a deep breath, she lowered her hands and

lifted her chin. "I had dinner at his house the night you switched shifts with Jeffrey. We fooled around a little."

"How many bases did he get?"

Glaring, she stood, knocking the chair to the floor. "He did not make a homerun, if that's what you're concerned about."

Lionel froze with his mouth agape. She had let Elliot touch her all over. Who cared if she stopped short of intercourse? He struggled to breathe. "Why? Why did you let him do that to you?"

She shrugged, folding her arms over her chest. "Everything happened so fast. We were talking, and then we weren't."

"Did this event happen because I can't get it up on demand anymore?"

"No." She threw open her arms. "It happened because you've neglected me for this pregnant employee who means more to you than your own wife."

He sprung to his feet. "I'm not fucking Michelle."

"You don't have to fuck to cheat."

Shaking, he pointed toward the garage door. "Damn you, woman, get out of my house."

"I own the house and the store." She pounded a fist into her open palm. "I'm not leaving."

"Neither am I." He fumed.

Noelle barked, standing between them.

Cowed into silence, he listened to his heavy pulse ringing in his ears. His beloved wife had almost slept with another man out of jealousy. How could he forgive her? "I'm done with dinner. I'll spend the night on the couch."

"No, sugar, you take the bed. Your arthritis will act up if you sleep down here." She pointed toward Noelle.

"You take her outside one last time, and I'll clean up and sleep on the sofa."

For a long moment, he waited.

She bagged up the leftovers. The seams of her pants strained against her hips when she leaned over the table.

Some part of him wanted to pull her into his arms and hold her tight. Who thought of his arthritis during a fight? But then an image of her bent over another man's kitchen table with his hands on the curve of her hips burned acid in his throat. How could he ever find her attractive again?

Chapter Nineteen

With a hand tucked under her cheek, Geraldine stared at the ghostly shadows in the living room. Unable to sleep after her fight with Lionel, she replayed the tape over and over in her mind, stopping at the right moments to punish herself again. Why had she told him the truth, the whole truth, and nothing but the truth? She had only intended to spin the events in her favor. How had she let her plan spool out of control?

The ceiling creaked from Lionel shifting in the bed. He must be turning from one side to the other, searching for a spot that eased the pain in his hip. Some part of her wanted to run upstairs and slip into the bed beside him, pushing her breasts against his back and wrapping her arms around his chest, erasing the bad memories of the evening with the healing magic of touch.

She groaned and shuddered. That's how she ended in this situation, letting another man touch her. Why couldn't she have brushed Elliot's hand from her thigh? Why couldn't she have grabbed her purse and left instead of letting him carry her into his bedroom and toss her onto the mattress and press the length of his body against hers? Why didn't she reject his dinner invitation? Why didn't she destroy his contact information? Why didn't she stop all of this nonsense before everything accelerated past the limits she could control?

Closing her eyes, she focused on her breath. She needed to find a way to sleep. Tugging the blankets close, she snuggled deep into the hard cushions, pushing out all thoughts, all worries, and all troubles. The squeaking mattress settled and the gentle snores of her husband rumbled like thunder in her ears. Warm, wet tears streamed down her cheeks.

Suddenly, she understood why her father needed her to keep his secret—what her mother didn't know couldn't hurt her. If she had kept her mouth shut, she would not have ripped apart the fabric of her marriage. Turning onto her back, the seams of the sofa as hard as a ridge of rocks, she stared at the ceiling. No, telling him didn't matter. The breach occurred as soon as she fell in love with the illusion of happiness captured in the smile of another man. With the fantasy over, she lay in the fractured terrain of reality, wondering if she could repair the damage or if it was too late.

****

When the alarm rang from his cell phone, Lionel rolled over and swiped the screen for an extra five minutes to snooze. Lying on his side, he stared at the cold, empty space beside him where his wife's sumptuous curves would normally be. Memories of their fight drifted to the surface of his thoughts, and he shoved them away, ignoring the raw feeling in his arms and legs.

Noelle stirred by his feet.

"You hungry, ol' girl?" The alarm sounded again. He sat, swung his legs over the side of the mattress, and swiped a finger to silence it. A dull ache throbbed in his lower back. An unexpected thrill of gratitude warmed his hands. Oh, how much worse that ache would be if he had slept on the sofa.

Walking beside Noelle, he descended the stairs. He paused on the threshold of the living room to snatch a glimpse of his sleeping wife. But the blankets were neatly folded and stacked on top of the pillow, and the curtains were open with the sunlight streaming into the unoccupied room. Turning, he padded into the kitchen. A waft of rich, roasting coffee filled his senses.

With her back toward him, Geraldine stood at the kitchen sink dressed in her outfit from last night. The buzzer dinged, and she poured a cup of coffee into her favorite mug.

Without a word, he opened the cupboard, removed the dog food, and filled a measuring cup with kibbles. He bent, tipping the food into the dog dish and hearing the *plink-plink-plink* of the morsels tinging against the steel sides.

Noelle buried her snout in the dish, sniffing and snuffling.

Geraldine grabbed another mug from the cupboard, poured coffee, and extended her arm.

When her fingers brushed against his, he winced. Nodding his thanks, he sipped the bitter brew.

Standing side by side in silence, he wondered who would break the stalemate first.

****

He's leaving. Geraldine rushed out into the garage. Slipping her purse over her shoulder, she tapped her knuckles on the passenger side window of the truck. Wooziness engulfed her body.

Over the rumbling engine, Lionel flashed a sidelong glance.

She rattled the door handle, and then knocked on the window again. She didn't have to be at work until eleven, but she did not want to linger on the deck drinking a second cup of coffee, dwelling on everything she could not change. If too much time and space built between them, then the chance of reconciliation grew slimmer. The survival of their relationship depended on the generosity of his presence.

Glowering, he unlocked the doors to the truck.

She flashed a grateful smile, climbing into the cab and tugging the seat belt across her chest. The air smelled of gasoline and the lavender soap Lionel used in the shower. Instinctively, she wanted to place her hand on the rough denim of his thigh, but she smoothed her sweaty palms against her lap and waited.

He shifted into Reverse and backed the truck out of the garage into the misty morning light. Turning, he drove through the maze of streets to the store in silence. Pulling into the lot, he stopped and leaned forward, squinting.

Geraldine followed his gaze to a red sports car idling toward the back of the lot.

A young man with a black braid stood beside the open driver's side door, grabbing Michelle's shoulders. She wrenched away, turning toward the loading dock, and he seized her wrist and yanked her back.

Indignation burned in the pit of Geraldine's stomach. *Oh, how dare he hurt her? She's pregnant.*

Lionel swerved into the nearest slot and threw the gear into Park. Opening the door, he hopped out of the cab and grabbed one of his bats from the bed of the pickup truck. "You leave her alone, you hear me?" He strode toward the couple, who were entangled in a battle, and lifted the bat toward his shoulder. Taking aim at the young man, he swung.

The young man released Michelle's arm and ducked into the car. The bat landed on the roof. The thwack of wood on metal reverberated across the parking lot.

Fear ricocheted inside her, and Geraldine jumped in her seat inside the truck.

The young man ground the gears. The tires spun against the gravel before propelling into Reverse.

Lionel shoved Michelle toward the loading dock before the car drove past them. Lifting the bat, Lionel chased the car across the lot until the young man swerved onto the street. Panting, he tossed the bat onto the ground. "No wonder I keep striking out. I can't even hit a guy as big as a tree."

Geraldine opened the truck's door. With trembling hands and legs, she fumbled down the step and wobbled on the pavement. Glancing from Lionel to Michelle, she wondered who to approach first.

Grumbling, Lionel stamped his feet back and forth across the pavement. He shook his fists at the sky and mumbled before stooping to retrieve the bat.

On the loading dock, Michelle shuddered with her arms wrapped around her waist.

Was she hurt? Geraldine ran over to soothe her. "Sugar, are you okay?" She scanned the girl's tear-streaked, wide-eyed face and searched her arms for bruises. "Let's go upstairs, and I'll show you to your new home." Glancing over her shoulder, she witnessed Lionel standing in the center of the parking lot, taking practice swings at an invisible ball. Shaking her head, she ushered Michelle up the stairs to the studio apartment.

In the kitchen, Geraldine pulled out a chair at the bistro table, filled the kettle with water, and set it on the stove to boil. Taking down two mugs from the cupboard, she set them on the table and dropped chamomile teabags into them.

Michelle slumped in the chair. "You don't have to do this." She pointed toward the mugs and the kettle.

"Oh, sugar, I want to." Geraldine patted Michelle's shoulder. "I saw what happened from the truck." She waved a hand. "Your boyfriend's lucky Lionel's not a good shot. He might have left with a broken jaw and not just a dented hood."

Staring at her hands, Michelle nodded. "I know you're being nice, but I don't think you really like me." She lifted her head and raised her eyebrows. "Why don't you like me?"

With the truth, Geraldine stiffened. The kettle whistled, and she snapped off the stove then poured the hot water into the mugs. After setting the kettle on the burner, she took the seat beside Michelle and dunked the teabag in the mug of hot water, watching the steam rise and curl. The girl was right, she didn't like her, but she was hospitable by habit. She tugged her lips into a straight line. "I don't know if Lionel told you, but I was pregnant once."

Michelle nodded. "I said he would have been a great dad." She swiveled toward the table and cupped the mug.

"Did he tell you the whole story?" Geraldine arched an eyebrow, studying the girl.

Frowning, Michelle shrugged.

Sighing, Geraldine sank back against the chair. She

squeezed her eyes shut for a second, gathering her strength to retell this sad story. Her heartbeat fluttered in her chest, and she wiped her moist palms against her thighs. Opening her eyes, she swallowed the tightness in her throat. "I was older than you, a little over thirty, and pregnant after months of trying. Lionel was over-the-moon-happy, especially when he found out I was carrying twins. He was the one who picked out all the items on the baby shower registry. Each night he read aloud a chapter from *What to Expect When You're Expecting*."

She smiled wistfully and blew on the steaming mug before taking a sip of the weak tea. "He wanted so badly to be a father. I almost felt terrible for making him wait so long." Remembering, she bowed her head. "But something went wrong, and I started getting contractions weeks before the twins were due. I called the hospital and described what I was feeling. The doctor on duty thought I was experiencing Braxton Hicks, basically fake contractions, and recommended I stay in bed with my feet propped up until my next appointment."

Breathing in deeply, she heaved her shoulders. "I didn't listen. I went to the store to make sandwiches as usual, sitting on the stool when I got tired. I didn't tell Lionel about my conversation with the doctor. He thought I was just working through a regular long day." She twisted her lips and blinked. Panic rose in her chest, and her hands shook. She placed aside the mug and brushed the hair from her eyes. "My water broke that afternoon. Lionel rushed me to the hospital, but it was too late. I went into labor, and the twins were born too soon." She choked on a sob and rubbed the back of her hand against her closed eyes. "Lionel never forgave me for what happened. The twins died within twenty-four hours."

"I'm sorry for your loss," Michelle said. "I didn't know the whole story. Only what Lionel told me."

"What did he tell you?" Geraldine lifted her face.

"He said I reminded him of his daughter."

Rapid knocks pounded against the door.

The twins would have been the same age. Did Lionel wish their daughter would have been just like Michelle? Geraldine jumped, pivoting toward the sound.

After standing, Michelle strode across the room and opened the door.

Lionel stepped inside, his face flushed and his shoulders slumped. He glanced at Geraldine, taking in the scene of the mugs of tea, and then into Michelle's face. "Are you okay?"

Michelle nodded. "Geraldine was telling me about the twins." She swallowed. "I'm sorry you lost them."

He heaved a sigh. "Well, that's all in the past now, isn't it? Right now, we need to make sure you're fine. That he didn't hurt you. That the baby's okay." He steered her back to the kitchen. "Did you file the domestic violence report with the tribal police?"

She shook her head. "I didn't have time."

"I don't want to hear any more excuses. You're filing the report now." He removed his cell phone and dialed. "Hope, sorry to wake you, but it's urgent. I need you to come to the store and take Michelle to the tribal police to file a domestic violence report." He gritted his teeth. "That son of a bitch was harassing her this morning outside the store. If I hadn't arrived when I did, he would have left her for dead." The muscles in his face softened. "Thanks." Ending the call, he shoved the phone into his pocket and frowned. "She'll be here in twenty minutes. Don't worry about starting late. This business is more important than work."

Geraldine bristled at her husband's parental words, but she nodded in agreement. "You need to protect yourself, sugar. We'll pay you for your missed hours."

Glancing from one to the other, Michelle clasped her hands to her chest. "I'm so thankful I listened to the Great Spirit." She smiled. "I'm so grateful for you both. You've been like family." She opened her arms and drew them into a shared embrace.

Breathing in the sage of Michelle's hair and the lavender soap on Lionel's skin, Geraldine sighed. The tightness in her chest loosened. Grief, longing, and jealousy melted away, leaving a residue of peace.

Chapter Twenty

Throughout the day, Lionel's internal weather report fluctuated between flashes of anger and lulls of grief, and lightning bolts of hatred and thundershowers of depression. During a moment of calm, he sent a group text message to Cassidy and Nick, asking them to meet him outside Jasper's Bar and Grill at six o'clock. He wanted to talk to them and get their opinion before he assessed how to proceed with his domestic situation.

Cassidy was the first to respond.

—*Can't get out tonight. I have Adam. Deb is meeting with the altar society at church.*—

Slumping against a stack of boxes in the sweltering warehouse, Lionel typed.

—*GG cheated. I don't know what to do.*—

—*No way. I'll ask Stephanie if she can watch Adam. Don't do anything stupid.*—

After wiping the sweat from his forehead, Lionel tucked his phone into his pocket and strode back into the store. He was supposed to be training one of the new hires about inventory control, but he couldn't focus. Every time he witnessed his wife smiling too brightly or standing too close or laughing too hard with a customer, he twisted his gut with worry.

Michelle strolled over and placed a hand on his forearm. "You don't look good. What's bothering you?"

He thumbed toward his wife, standing in the deli section. "We've been fighting over how much I care about you."

Frowning, she slid her hand toward his wrist. Entwining her fingers through his, she squeezed his hand. "Everything should be better now. I understand why she hated me."

Shaking his head, he tugged free his hand. "It's not you. It's her. She cheated on me."

Michelle gasped and swung her head in Geraldine's direction.

From his pocket, his phone pinged. He removed the phone and swiped the screen to read the message from Nick.

—*Can't meet at six. I have an afternoon meeting with the mayor I can't cancel. How about six-thirty?*—

Quickly, Lionel typed.

—*Fine. Works for me.*—

Cassidy responded.

—*Works for me, too.*—

Lionel tucked the phone into his pocket.

"Your wife still loves you." Michelle tilted her head. "She would not be nice to me if she did not love you."

He bristled, tugging his lips into a frown. "Great sentiment, kid, but you don't even know how to manage your life."

She shoved back her shoulders and straightened her lips. "I might not have your experience, but I know the Great Spirit never lies."

Oh, no. Not the witchy, voodoo stuff. Lionel cringed.

"There is a Wapi saying, the stick that does not

break grows stronger." She pointed toward Geraldine who winked, passing a wrapped sandwich to a customer. "She is still here. She has not broken. She is stronger." Turning toward Lionel, she pointed at his chest. "Now, it is up to you. Do you want to break? Or do you want to grow stronger?"

He fumed. "You're just a kid." He pointed toward the registers. "Go check."

For one long moment, she held his gaze before she strode toward the checkout line and opened a register.

Heaving a sigh, Lionel stalked toward the warehouse. Slashing aside the plastic curtain, he strode out on the loading dock into the light. Squinting, he crossed his arms and stared out at the fields, wondering if his world would ever be right again.

****

Several hours later, the lunchtime crowd shuffled into the deli. Geraldine relaxed, even as the line snaked around the counter. Greeting customers with false smiles and making sandwiches to order lulled her into a predictable rhythm that calmed her nerves. Glancing up every now and then, she tried to catch Lionel's gaze. But he would not acknowledge her. She shivered. Had she ceased to exist?

When the lunchtime crowd dispersed, a quiet hush fell over the deli. Geraldine wiped down the counters, whistling off-key. If she kept occupied, then she wouldn't have to dwell on anything. Would she?

"Call for Geraldine on line four," Michelle said over the public address system.

Geraldine set aside the damp cloth and removed her plastic gloves. After punching the hold button and the number four, she placed the phone against her ear.

"Geraldine, speaking, how may I help you?"

"It's Hope. Deb told me what happened." She paused. "How are you doing?"

Geraldine flattened her lips. How could Deb share her secret? Shifting her weight to one hip, she tucked one hand under her armpit and leaned against the counter. Thankfully, no customers stood before her. She didn't want to anyone to overhear this conversation. "Not so well. Lionel and I aren't speaking."

"The redwoods survive because their roots intertwine like linked hands."

Not another Wapi saying. Geraldine frowned. She hated those obtuse maxims almost as much as Lionel did. "What do redwoods have to do with my situation, sugar?"

Hope sighed. "When was the last time you and Lionel had sex?"

Heat invaded her cheeks, and Geraldine pivoted toward the wall, not wanting anyone to see or hear. "We try all the time and fail, but that's only part of the problem."

"What's the other part?"

Glancing over her shoulder, Geraldine confirmed no one was eavesdropping. "Michelle," she hissed.

"How can I help? I already accompanied her to the tribal police. She filed a domestic violence report. I asked her if she needed a place to stay, but she said you and Lionel already made arrangements. Is that true?"

Geraldine grumbled. "We're letting her stay in the warehouse loft that used to be our office."

"Why don't you bring her to me? I'll take care of her." Hope paused. "I think I have a solution for your other problem. I'll drop off a Lover's Pie on your doorstep on my way to the tribal meeting this afternoon. One slice is all he needs."

Geraldine bit her lower lip, narrowing her gaze. Hope came up with all sorts of strange concoctions that sometimes smelled and tasted worst than garbage, even if they worked. "What's in it?"

"Some roots to help with the problems older men encounter with their sex life. Don't worry. It's completely safe. My people have used it for ages...long before white men invented all those drugs with nasty side effects."

Geraldine laughed. "Lionel won't take them anymore for precisely those reasons."

"Lover's Pie has no side effects."

Twirling the long phone cord around her wrist, Geraldine dropped her gaze. "Why are you so intent on helping me?"

"Isn't that what friends are for?"

Geraldine warmed with gratitude. She tilted her head to the side. "There's something more, isn't there?"

Hope inhaled deeply. "The love you and Lionel have is so much bigger than you realize. From my experience, I know staying in love is hard. Long-term love requires faith, fortitude, and forgiveness. Richard and I had that kind of love." She sighed. "Don't get me wrong. Nick is great, but he's not Richard. We don't share years of history. Do you understand?"

Geraldine shrugged, releasing the phone cord from around her wrist. "When you're older and have more to lose, divorce is harder."

"That's not what I'm saying. You and Lionel are like Richard and me. I know what you have, and I know how much I value what you have. I miss that type of love you take for granted because you assume it will always be there because it always has. That's why I called. As selfish as it sounds, I can't afford to have you lose that kind of love." She hitched her breath. "Watching you lose Lionel would feel like losing Richard all over again."

Hearing Hope's gentle sobs triggered a new level of respect and compassion for her friend. Her life wasn't perfect. Nick's money didn't solve every problem. Richard's love was lost because it had died with him. "Thank you, Hope."

She sniffled. "Don't thank me. Thank the Great Spirit."

After ending the call, Geraldine stared off across the distance of the store, focusing on nothing in particular. Nausea roiled the contents in her stomach. She sank onto a stool, wrapped her arms around her waist, and wondered when this whole nightmare would be over.

Chapter Twenty-One

That night, Lionel paced back and forth in front of his truck parked a few spaces away from the glittering lights of Jasper's Bar and Grill. He shook a fist into the cool evening air. "That man can't get away with messing with my wife *and* messing up my life." He pointed at Nick. "I blame you, too."

"Me?" Scowling, Nick lurched to his feet from where he slumped against the truck's bumper. "Your wife's affair with Old Red has nothing to do with me."

"You gave him the loan to open a business here." Lionel jabbed a finger at Nick's chest. "You could have denied him money and sent him packing to the next city."

Cassidy leaned against the streetlight, his hands thrust into his pockets. "I'm so glad I'm not involved." He glanced at Lionel. "Just don't ask me to beat up Nick. He's in better shape than me."

His chest heaving, Lionel stood between the two men. Who would betray him next? Heat rushed to his face. He glowered at Nick. "Why did you and GG leave the table around the same time the other night and return together? Were you having a tryst?"

Lifting his eyebrows, Nick threw open his arms. "I was in the kitchen and saw her on the deck. I wandered out to see what was bugging her." He shook his head and dropped his arms to the sides. "We took a walk and talked about our fathers, how they both disappointed us, but how we didn't have to disappoint ourselves because we could choose to be different people than the ones who left us their legacy." He took a step forward. "I wasn't asking Geraldine to have a wild affair. I already have more than I can handle at home."

Cassidy snickered. "I wouldn't mind a wild love affair if it lasted precisely one week."

Frowning, Lionel pivoted to face his friend. "Why one week?"

Cassidy tilted his head, gazing at the darkening sky. "Just enough memories to last a lifetime and the longest I could be away from home on a job site because of my childcare agreement."

Nick chuckled. "I don't think you'd be getting much work done."

Tossing back his sandy curls, Cassidy smiled. "Oh, but she'd be working a lot on me."

Lionel refused to join in the laughter. As a cuckold, he didn't appreciate the banter.

Nick kicked a pebble on the sidewalk into the gutter. "So, LJ, what do you want us to do?"

Bouncing on his heels, Cassidy punched a fist into his open palm. "Elliot's smaller and scrawnier than me. I can pull him over the bar and beat him up—just like when we were in college and that guy hit on Geraldine at the bar across from the university."

Remembering, Lionel dropped his head into his hands. "She was flirting with the bastard." He lifted his head, and his eyes flashed. "What was the guy supposed to do? Ignore her?"

A crooked smile tilted on Nick's face. "Hell, I'm lucky I never made a pass at your woman, or you both would have roughed me up."

Frowning, Lionel narrowed his gaze. "You had enough women dripping off your arms that you didn't need to make a pass at my girl."

"True." Grinning, Nick ran a hand through his dark hair.

Cassidy glanced at the marquee above the restaurant. "So, what are we supposed to do? Stand here all night and debate our options?"

Shaking his head, Nick strode toward the door. "I don't know about you two, but I'm ordering a drink."

Lionel followed Nick and Cassidy inside to the light and laughter of the bar. The warmth of the room wrapped around him like a snug coat. What if Elliot wasn't working tonight? Would he have the courage to return at another time and confront the man about what he had done with his wife?

Nick waved to the hostess. "Just drinks tonight." He motioned for the men to follow him to the bar. He weaved around a couple and found three stools. Taking the middle seat, he patted the counter. "I'm paying."

Cassidy chuckled. "You always pay."

"Not always." Lionel took the seat closest to the door. "Sometimes I pay."

"You only pay because you strike out at bat." Nick arched an eyebrow.

Another wave of humiliation crashed over Lionel. How could he have missed hitting Paul's head? He was aiming for the guy's face, as big as a melon, and the guy ducked quicker than he could swing. He shook his head. How could his skills have deteriorated so quickly through the years? He used to hit better than Nick, cracking the bat so hard against the ball that it soared over the fence and bounced across the parking lot. Sighing, he opened and closed his hands, the joints slow and stiff.

"Good evening, gentlemen. What shall I get you tonight?" Elliot flashed a smile and winked.

At the sound of Elliot's smooth voice, Lionel tensed his jaw. *You charming, cheating bastard*, he wanted to scream. But he swallowed the words.

Nick waved to the men beside him. "Three beers on tap, whichever brand you recommend." He smiled, and a dimple creased his cheek. "We're celebrating."

"Oh, really?" Elliot grabbed a mug and poured the first beer. "What's the occasion?"

"The last night drinking here." Nick folded his arms on the counter. "Remember that loan you signed?"

Lionel leaned closer. Nick would really call the loan due, wouldn't he? A warm gush of loyalty washed over him.

Pouring the second beer, Elliot nodded.

Nick tapped his fingers against the counter. "Well, there's a little clause on the final page about the morality of the establishment and that includes the character of the owner and the employees."

Frowning, Elliot set three beers on the counter. "I don't understand."

Lionel huffed, balling a hand into a fist. "You tried to screw my wife."

Stepping back from the counter, Elliot widened his eyes and dropped his hands. "She told you?"

"Everything." Lionel huffed.

Cassidy thumped a fist into his palm. "We can settle it out back, if you prefer."

Raising his arms, Elliot shook his head. "Listen, we

only had a bit of fun. She told me she didn't want it to happen again."

The seething anger venting off Lionel's skin cooled. She didn't pursue him like he feared. He uncurled his fist, shaking out the stiff joints. She also had enough sense to not encourage the man. But he couldn't be guaranteed anything, could he? He narrowed his gaze. "It better not happen again."

"I'm sorry." Elliot dropped his arms and paced. "I didn't mean to hurt anyone. I know your wife didn't, either. She felt really bad about what happened."

"How did it happen?" Lionel breathed in quickly. Why was he asking? Did he really want to know all the gory details? He slouched on the stool, staring at his untouched beer. Maybe he should leave. What was he hoping to accomplish here?

Elliot grabbed a towel and wiped down the counter. "Neither one of us had plans that night. I invited her over for dinner." He slowed his movements and smiled. "We talked."

"How do you go from talking to sex?" A vein throbbed in Lionel's forehead.

Frowning, Elliot tossed aside the towel. "Have you talked to your wife lately? She's a great listener. She's also very caring." He slumped against the register. "You're a lucky man."

Lionel curled his hand around the mug of beer and took a sip of the cold, bitter fluid. "I don't feel lucky. I feel used."

Elliot pointed to his chest. "I'm the one who should be feeling that way, not you." He waved a finger at Lionel. "You get to come home to her every night. She gets to listen to your stories, laugh at your jokes, and sleep in your bed." He crossed his arms over his chest and blinked several times. "She wouldn't even let me undress her. She wanted to go home to you."

Heat and anger radiated off Elliot's skin. Lionel bowed his head, processing the man's words. All this time he believed Elliot had taken advantage of Geraldine's flirtatious nature. But the truth was Geraldine had used Elliot for the attention she wasn't getting at home. Hot shame doused him, and he gulped another mouthful of bitter beer. She was right. He was too consumed with concern about Michelle. That reason didn't excuse her behavior, but it illuminated the larger problem. Lionel hadn't talked to his wife in a long time about anything that mattered—his struggle with erectile dysfunction, his declining ability to play softball, and his overwhelming need to parent. He had only talked about his grief over the twins when pressured about his interest in Michelle. He set down the mug of beer and grumbled. Was it too late to fix this situation?

"Listen, I care about Geraldine." Elliot stepped closer. "She's a fabulous woman. But if you don't start treating her that way, she'll end up leaving for a man who makes her feel fabulous again." He opened his arms and shook his head. "I just hope if she does leave, you won't be angry if I ask to see her again."

"Of course, I'd be angry." Lionel slapped a hand on the counter. "If anyone is leaving, that person is me." He pointed to his chest.

The doors opened, and a burst of people flocked to the far end of the bar.

Elliot excused himself to take care of them.

Lionel hung his head low. "All these years I've been faithful." He took a long sip of bitter beer and stared into the mug. "I deserve a faithful wife."

"She made a mistake." Nick patted his back. "Do you want me to call Elliot's loan due?"

How could Nick call infidelity a mistake? A mistake was an error made unintentionally. Lionel thought back to when Geraldine told him the truth— how nervous she was, fiddling with the straw, and saying her last conversation with Elliot made her feel uncomfortable. Sure, she avoided his gaze, but she also said she loved Lionel. She just felt old and neglected, worse than Noelle whom they coddled like a child rather than a geriatric dog. Elliot made her feel alive and chosen. That's why she took her flirtation too far. He swallowed another mouthful of beer. When was the last time either of them felt alive and chosen in their marriage? Shaking his head, he couldn't remember.

"LJ, did you hear me?"

Raising his head, Lionel met Nick's gaze. "Yeah, you asked if you should call Elliot's loan due." In that scenario, Elliot would have to pay back the money in full or default and lose the business. The possibility of driving Geraldine's lover out of town appealed to his baser instincts, but a larger concern bloomed. If she cheated with Elliot, why wouldn't she cheat with someone else? He couldn't exactly ask Nick to run everyone out of town. "No, don't. That won't solve the problem."

Cassidy nudged Lionel's shoulder. "I could still take him out back and rough him up."

The image of Elliot's face beaten to a pulp filled Lionel with momentary satisfaction. But once the bruises faded and the scabs healed, he would be free to roam around town without a visual reminder of his indiscretion. Lionel rubbed his face with a hand. He didn't want to use his friend to bully another man, especially after he fought to stop Michelle's boyfriend from beating her. Violence didn't solve anything. "No, thanks." He finished the beer and stood, taking out his wallet and leaving a ten on the counter. "I think I have to solve this one myself."

"How?" Nick shifted on the stool.

Lionel glanced down the bar at Elliot joking with the new set of customers and witnessed the man through his wife's eyes—funny, delightful, and engaging. He stiffened. When was the last time he made his wife laugh? Coldness plunged through his body. He couldn't remember. After swiveling toward his friends, he placed a hand on each man's shoulder. Determination steeled his jaw. No more avoidance through silence and posturing. "I need to go home and talk to my wife."

****

Buzzing with energy, Geraldine cinched the robe tight around her waist and hunched close to the computer monitor in her home office after her shift at the deli. She was spying on the store. Lionel hadn't told her where he was headed after he dropped her off after work. The silence stretched taut between them, as solid as the twin gold bands they wore, promising to bind them separately together. But after three hours staring at the screen without any movement, she prickled with fear. Where was her husband if he wasn't at the store with Michelle?

Noelle slumbered at her feet, snoring.

Stretching her arms overhead, Geraldine yawned. The clock on the computer monitor read ten o'clock.

Maybe she should try to sleep.

The garage door rattled up, and Lionel's truck rumbled in.

Noelle lifted her head and barked.

A zing of excitement tingled through her body. *He's home.* Standing, Geraldine stamped her feet against the carpet, pounding feeling back into them. She leaned over to switch off the monitor. A shape shifted on the screen, catching her attention. Peering closer, she squinted at someone throwing a bucket of fluid against the wall. The figure tossed something. An explosion of light filled the screen followed by the flicker of flames. She jolted, and the figure darted out of camera range.

With her heartbeat thumping in her chest, she lunged for the landline beside the keyboard. She punched in the number, thinking of Michelle trapped in the studio apartment above the warehouse. Lionel's footsteps climbed the stairs, echoing like the blood pounding in her ears.

He stood in the doorway, his broad shoulders filling the space and blocking out the hallway light. He smelled of sweat and alcohol like he had played a game of softball and drank a six pack. "I need to talk to you."

Lifting her hand, she motioned for him to be silent. "Not now."

"Yes, now." He stepped into the room. "What I have to say is more important than talking with your girlfriends."

The sound of the dispatcher filled her other ear.

"Nine-one-one, what is your emergency?"

"Someone just started a fire at Larry's Deli, and another person is trapped upstairs." She rattled off the address, her voice trembling almost as much as her hands.

Lionel raised his eyebrows before turning and bounding down the stairs.

She rushed to follow him, jerking the cord. The phone crashed to the floor.

Noelle yelped.

Geraldine squatted, lifting the phone and setting it back on the desk. Oh, why hadn't she called from her cell phone?

"Ma'am, are you okay?"

The disembodied voice of the dispatcher startled her. "Yes, I'm fine. I just dropped the phone."

"The fire department and the paramedics are on their way."

After hanging up the receiver, Geraldine stepped around Noelle and darted down the stairs. "Lionel, stop!" By the time she stepped into the garage, the truck had already lumbered out of the driveway, its headlights cutting across her body before the garage door sealed shut.

Breathless, she stood in the puddle of light from the rafters, dressed in her nightgown and slippers. Conflicting emotions whipped through her body like a fierce wind.

Damn him, leaving to save the girl.

Good for him, leaving to save their business.

Chapter Twenty-Two

Speeding through the dark night, Lionel gripped the steering wheel. Darting across intersections through yellow lights, he propelled the truck forward, only one goal in mind. He needed to save Michelle. Fear tightened his throat. He couldn't lose another baby. Blinking to clear his blurred vision, he accelerated. He couldn't endure the pain a second time. Tightness squeezed his chest. The loss would kill him.

One block away, he spied a column of smoke climbing toward the bruised sky. He steered right onto the familiar street and slammed on the brakes. The truck skidded to a stop. The stink of burned rubber filled the cab. A crowd of people had gathered to watch the firefighters shower streams of water against the dance of flames burning through the store.

After pulling over to the nearest curb, Lionel parked, released his seat belt, and threw open the door. Ignoring the aches in his joints, he jumped to the pavement and ran, pushing past strangers toward the yellow tape roping off the store's parking lot. From the back of the store, a flicker of orange light danced across the rooftop. The second story was engulfed in flames. He gasped. The stink of charred wood and melted plastic choked his lungs.

"Sir, you need to stay back." A fireman extended his arm, blocking the path. "We need space to work."

"Michelle's in there." He pointed toward the second story window. Even from this distance, the heat of the flames lapped his face. "She's pregnant. You need to save her and the baby." Emotion strained his voice. "Please."

The firefighter nodded. "Sir, she's fine." Gesturing to the left, the firefighter strode toward the ambulance parked beside the curb.

A woman huddled on the step of the open doors, a blanket wrapped around her shoulders.

Tension released from his shoulders, and he rushed toward her. "Michelle!"

Glancing up, she smiled. "Lionel."

He knelt beside her, stroking her hair. "What happened?"

She shook her head. "I was sleeping. There was an explosion. Then fire." She pointed toward the store. "The firefighters broke the door and carried me downstairs."

Hugging her close, he let the tears fall. "I'm so glad you're safe." He sighed. "I'm so glad the baby's safe."

"Me, too." She released him, glancing over his shoulder. "Where's Geraldine?"

Chagrin tingled across his face. "I left her at home."

"Why?" She frowned. "Does she still hate me?"

"No, she's the one who called 911." If she had hung up when he had asked to talk with her, who knows what would have happened? Fresh shame doused him. Standing, he winced as the joints in his knees and back creaked with pain. He waved toward the paramedic. "Does she need to see a doctor?"

The paramedic stepped close and glanced over his notes. "We're just keeping her to make sure she does not go into shock." He squatted beside Michelle and checked her pulse and flashed a light into her eyes. Standing, he nodded. "She should be fine to go. If her skin gets cold and clammy or her pulse races, take her to the emergency room."

"Will do." Lionel offered Michelle his arm.

Standing, she returned the blanket to the paramedic and linked her arm through his. "Where are you taking me?" She bowed her head. "I can't return to Paul."

"Don't worry." Lionel tugged her close. No way would he ever let Paul near her again. He coughed from the rancid smoke. Doubt clouded his thoughts. Maybe he should ask Geraldine first. A quick glance at Michelle's furrowed brow wiped away his fears. If needed, he would deal with Geraldine's resistance. "You can come to my house."

****

When the garage door rattled up, Geraldine rushed into the kitchen and flung open the door, watching the truck trundle into the space. She clasped her hands against her chest and exhaled. He was safe. He was home. She stepped into the garage and waited, eager to toss her arms around his neck and pull him close for a hug.

Lionel shut off the engine and opened the door. He shuffled around the back of the truck to the passenger's side and helped Michelle out.

Anger stiffened her smile. Was Lionel expecting them to house Michelle now that the studio was gone and she had nowhere else to go?

"We're safe, but the store's not."

Lionel smelled charred, like a barbecue of chemicals.

Wincing, Geraldine held the door.

"Thank you for saving me." Michelle lifted her face and smiled. "Lionel told me you called 911."

That radiant smile, so full of gratitude, tugged at the resistance building around Geraldine's heart. "Oh, sugar, anyone would have." She brushed away the statement. "Let's get you showered and changed, okay? I think I have something that will fit you."

Lionel walked past her into the house. The floorboards in the kitchen and dining room creaked before he headed up the stairs.

Geraldine bit her lower lip, resisting the urge to trail after him and demand to know how long he promised Michelle she could stay. Turning, she waved Michelle toward the downstairs bathroom. "Fresh towels are in the cabinet above the toilet. I'll leave the clothes outside the door." She climbed the stairs to the master bedroom and closed the door. Tensing her back, she listened to water plunk through the pipes in the shower. *Should I talk to him now or wait?*

Noelle snored at the foot of the bed.

Bending, Geraldine lifted Lionel's smoke-filled clothes out of the hamper and tossed them into the washing machine in the hallway. She wiggled her nose, trying to prevent a sneeze. Returning to the bedroom, she rifled through her drawers for a simple cotton nightgown for Michelle to wear.

Downstairs, she placed the nightgown beside the bathroom door before she strode into the living room and stripped the sheets off the sofa. With the bundle of old sheets tucked under her arm, she walked upstairs, placed them in the washer, and grabbed a clean set from the hall closet. She passed Michelle who followed her on her way to the living room. She tucked the fresh sheet into the corners of the sofa and smoothed out the blanket and fluffed the pillow, remembering how she had slept here last night under different circumstances.

Michelle stood by, saying nothing.

Geraldine finished. "You'll sleep here for tonight. We'll talk about tomorrow when it comes."

"Thank you." Michelle wrapped her arms around Geraldine's neck.

She smelled like Geraldine's favorite oatmeal-and-shea-butter soap. Her slim, tense body full of gratitude squeezed against Geraldine's bones. The hardness fractured, and Geraldine glimpsed a frightened young woman on the verge of creating a whole new life—both literally and figuratively. For the first time, she imagined that young woman as her child, her adult daughter, the one she lost and never had to raise and parent, protect, and love. Tears filled her eyes, and she sniffed. "You're welcome." She patted Michelle's back before she released her. "Sweet dreams, sugar. Good night." Geraldine grabbed Michelle's clothes and wet towel from the bathroom and climbed the stairs. Even though the swish and whirl of the washing machine would keep her awake, she started the load. How could she sleep when her entire life had burned down?

Lionel sat in bed with the tin of Lover's Pie in his lap, watching TV. "Our store is a special news report." He pointed.

After taking the remote out of his hand, she switched off the TV. Pain seized her chest. How could she watch her father's legacy be destroyed? Insurance only covered so much. What would they do for additional income? How would they pay for the furloughed employees? How long would rebuilding the store take? How would they occupy their time? Pain flooded her body. None of these questions would need to be answered if they hadn't allowed Michelle to stay in the studio, because no one would have burned down their store. She straightened her lips, wondering if she should tell Lionel the arsonist was Michelle's boyfriend.

That's right. The vengeful, young man had tossed lighter fluid on the back wall and lit a match.

While she waited for Lionel's return, she had sat in front of the computer, playing and replaying the surveillance videos from different camera angles until she identified him. Tomorrow she would forward the tapes to the police, but she had other things on her mind right now. She flicked on the Tiffany light, illuminating the room. She glanced at her husband propped against the pillows, chewing. The knot of pain unraveled in her chest, and relief wound through her body. No visible damage to his face and arms. She couldn't see his legs tucked beneath the sheets, but she suspected they, too, were fine. "Michelle can stay the night, but she can't live here. We need to give her to Hope. She belongs with her people."

Without glancing at his wife, Lionel nodded. "I know."

"Do you?" Geraldine set the remote on the nightstand and crossed her arms over her chest.

Lionel swallowed and pointed his fork toward the pie. "This is good. What is it?"

Narrowing her gaze, she spied the half-eaten tin in

his lap. The fragrant smells of the foreign recipe filled her lungs. "It's called Lover's Pie. It's Hope's recipe. I don't know what's in it, but I do know you're only supposed to have one slice." Worried too much of the concoction might spike his libido when she was not in the mood, she lunged for what was left.

Lionel raised the tin overhead. "I'll eat as much as I want. I'm hungry. I didn't have dinner."

Shaking her head, she sat up on her knees and seized the tin out of his hand. "No, you won't. If you eat the rest of that thing, you'll be hornier than a cow during mating season."

Frowning, he licked the fork. "You mean it's an aphrodisiac?"

"More like an erectile dysfunction meal."

Widening his eyes, he dropped the fork in the sheets. "You told her about my problem?"

She grabbed the fork and placed it in the pie tin. Standing, she pivoted toward the door. "I never need to tell that woman anything. She always seems to know."

"True." He chuckled. "She's seems really dialed in sometimes."

"No kidding." Geraldine nodded toward the door. She might not be frisky right now, but who knew how she would feel later? "I'll be right back. I need to refrigerate these leftovers, just in case the magic works." She winked. When she returned minutes later, she met his gaze. "Yes?"

He patted the space beside him. "I have a few things to say."

She skirted around the mattress, unfastened the sash on her kimono, and slipped under the covers to sit beside him.

Taking a deep breath, he knitted his hands together. "I went to Jasper's tonight to talk to Elliot about what happened."

A small intake of air caught in her lungs, and tension threaded down her legs.

"He said I shouldn't focus on the event but on the bigger picture." Pivoting, he focused his gaze. "He thinks you're a fabulous woman who deserves a man who recognizes how fabulous you are." He frowned. "I know I take you for granted. How can I not? We've been married for so long." He bowed his head and fiddled with the stitching on the sheet. "I always expected a certain level of trust and decency." Shaking his head from side to side, he crumpled the sheet into his fist. "Damn, it, GG, I know you are a flirt. I know you like excitement and danger. I just did not know you are capable of being like your father and taking things too far." He sighed. "I honestly don't know how we can recover." He covered his face with his hands. "How can I trust you again?"

"You can't." A weight settled in her chest. Shame and remorse singed her cheeks. She straightened her legs and leaned against the pillow. "I betrayed you. I'm not worthy of trust." Thinking, she bit her lower lip. "When I covered up my father's mistakes with lies, I thought I was protecting my mother. I believed I could save their marriage, but holding onto those lies destroyed the integrity of my life." She flared her nostrils. "I loved my father. I admired him. He was everything until I met you." She stuttered on a hitched breath. "Then he betrayed me with his lust. I took to heart I was no better than him and never would be." Swallowing the tears in her throat, she blinked. "I need constant validation, and that need has grown immensely since I've grown older." She ran her fingers over the skin above her chest. "I stayed slim, but everything else has withered like an overripe peach."

He held her hand. "I know how you feel. I miss the days when I could just think of you and I'd be ready to go. Now I touch you and kiss you, and nothing happens most of the time. I'm broken down there." He barked a dark laugh. "And don't even get me started on softball. I used to hit so well that ball would soar over the fence and bounce across the parking lot. Now I can't even hit a moving man's head as big as a melon." He squeezed her fingers. "I'm sorry, GG, for neglecting you. I know I put Michelle above our marriage with my fantasies of being a parent, even if the kid wasn't mine. Until recently, I never fully grieved the loss of the twins." He trembled. "Why did you give yourself to another man?"

"I did not *give myself* to him." She gritted her teeth. "I let him take more than he should have." Sighing, she shook her head. "The whole night was a big mistake. I'm sorry I failed you. I'll never go out with another man without you being there. I promise." She scooted closer and pressed the length of her leg against the warmth of his. Tilting her head, she breathed in the scent of lavender soap. She wanted to bury her face against his neck and inhale his essence until she dissolved. "I was weak. I never would have told you what had happened if you hadn't confronted me that night." She sighed. "In that moment, I had a choice—either lie to cover up my mistake like I had done for my father or come clean and accept the consequences." She placed her head on his shoulder. "Maybe I should have lied. We could have moved on as if nothing had ever happened."

"No, you did the right thing." He kissed her forehead. "I needed to know. I was so far gone in my obsession with Michelle's baby I needed the wake-up call, no matter how much the truth hurt."

She placed her other hand against the thud of his heartbeat. "Where do we go from here?"

"I don't know, dear."

A quiver of nervousness rippled throughout her body. Whenever she was stuck, she knew Lionel would find a way out. But he didn't have a plan. Oh, what would they do? For a minute, she rested against him, one hand clasped in his, the other against his chest.

Finally, he untangled his fingers from hers and nudged her head off his shoulder. He slid down against the mattress, his head resting on the pillow. Reaching up, he tugged her arm until she joined him, lying side by side, and facing each other. With a broad hand, he stroked the curve of her face from forehead to chin. "I think that pie's working."

The rough texture of his skin excited her nerves, and she curled her toes and closed her eyes. She did not expect the shock of his mouth on hers, his tongue parting her lips, with a kiss. *Oh, my, I'll have to ask Hope for that recipe.*

Chapter Twenty-Three

After a hearty breakfast, Lionel drove Michelle to Wapi Mountain to speak with Hope.

During the drive, Michelle rolled down the window and leaned into the wind. "I can smell the redwoods." She closed her eyes. "My mother used to tell me stories of the sacred mountain and how if you slept in a copse of trees facing north, the Great Spirit would visit you with dreams." Opening her eyes, she shifted toward Lionel and smiled. "Not just any dreams, but dreams that are real."

"Aren't all dreams real?" Lionel gave her a sidelong glance.

She shook her head. "No, most dreams mean nothing. These dreams tell the future."

"Prophetic dreams?" He scoffed. "Your whole nation is whacked out."

Frowning, she slapped her hands against her thighs. "Don't speak that way about my people."

Flicking another glance in her direction, he recognized the fierceness in her brown eyes. He tensed his jaw and returned his focus to the road. "I'm sorry if I offended you." Why was he always apologizing to women? He gripped the steering wheel tighter. "I don't have a religion."

"Dreams that are real are not a religion." Michelle huffed. "Those dreams are part of the Wapi Way of life."

Humph. A way of life. Like his life in the deli, stocking shelves, ringing up customers, building custom sandwiches, mopping floors, and cleaning windows. How would he spend his days while that life was rebuilt? Sighing, he drove up the paved road and lurched to the top of the mountain. He parked in the circular driveway and climbed out of the cab, arching his back and breathing in the fresh mountain air.

Michelle gaped at the surroundings, from the stone mansion to the views of the valley and the Wapi River. She clasped her hands to her chest. "I have never been on the sacred mountain." After placing her hands on her belly, she closed her eyes. "Feel the power, baby. Feel the power through your mama's hands. That is Father Earth calling to us." She opened her eyes and spread wide her arms. "We are home."

Lionel wrapped an arm around her shoulders and steered her toward the front door. He didn't want her to go running down the windy roads to find a copse of trees to take a nap in the hopes of receiving a message from the future.

A few birds darted overhead, twittering.

Michelle tracked them with her gaze.

He rang the doorbell and waited.

A few moments later, Hope opened the door and smiled. She wore another caftan dress. Bracelets *clacked* on her wrists. Her bare feet were unadorned. "Welcome." She ushered them into the foyer.

Michelle glanced around the wide space, taking in the Wapi artifacts. "My mother had a rug like that." She pointed to the runner along the hallway. "I watched her make it over a period of weeks. She tried to teach me once, but I had no patience to learn." Smiling, she patted her belly. "Maybe my daughter and I can learn together."

Frowning, Lionel released his arm from around her shoulders. "How do you know you're having a girl? We haven't even had a sonogram yet."

Hope chuckled, leading them toward the kitchen. "A mother always knows."

An intuitive mother always knows. Geraldine hadn't been in touch with her pregnancy. She didn't know they were having twins until the doctor discovered two sets of heartbeats.

"Have a seat." Hope waved toward the round table near the windows facing the backyard where Nick practiced batting.

Lionel clenched and unclenched his hands, remembering how he swung at Paul's head and missed. He took a seat next to Michelle and folded his hands on the table. "So, you know about our dilemma, right?"

Nodding, Hope poured three mugs of tea and carried them to the table. "Everyone knows the deli burned down last night. It's on the news."

"Yeah, well, Michelle was staying in the upstairs apartment. Now she has no place to go and no job." He cupped his hands around the warm, steaming mug. "Geraldine and I aren't in a position to house her, and Michelle can't return to Paul." He bent to sniff the faint aroma of lemons and mint. "I'm hoping you know of some place on the reservation where she can stay."

Hope sat beside him. When she cupped her mug in her hands, the bracelets on her wrists jangled. "If you hadn't been so stubborn and had listened to the Great Spirit, then none of these things would have happened."

"What things?" Lionel released the mug and sat back against the chair.

"Red." She waved a hand from her head to her heart to the rings on her fingers.

Michelle touched his arm and widened her eyes. "Why didn't you tell me you spoke with the Great Spirit?"

He gazed into her brown eyes and winced from a pinch of shame. Why did women hold so much power over him? He bowed his head and sighed. "I already told you I don't believe in any of this religious stuff."

"A message from the Great Spirit is not religious stuff." Michelle scrunched her face into a frown. "It's like someone calling you on the phone with important information and you hanging up on them."

Hope laughed, tossing back her long black hair.

Between the two women, Lionel was penned into a corner. He glanced outside, staring at Nick and willing him to come inside and save him.

"I'll help Michelle find housing and work." Hope patted Michelle's hand. "You'll also need to transfer your medical files to the clinic." She twisted her mouth. "I don't know how long it will take to set up things. But you are welcome to stay here in the meantime."

"Thank you." Michelle smiled, glancing from Hope to Lionel. "And the baby thanks you, too." She bowed her head toward her belly.

Standing, Lionel motioned to leave. "I need to get back home and take Geraldine to our appointment with the insurance adjuster."

Hope nodded. "Wait just a minute, and I'll walk you out." She smiled at Michelle. "Do you want to finish your tea or go up to see your room?"

Michelle gestured toward the window. "I want to go outside and be with the mountain, if you don't mind."

"No, I don't." Hope led her to the French doors overlooking the deck. "Just keep away from the batting cages. I'll come back and join you in a few minutes." Turning, she linked her arm through Lionel's and led him through the maze of rooms to the front door. "I know you think the Wapi Way is just a bunch of hocus-pocus, but the Great Spirit never lies." She stopped and faced him. "I know what Geraldine did. She's sorry. I know she won't do anything like it again."

"Is that what the Great Spirit told you?" He stepped back and broadened his stance. "Trying to seduce another man should not just be dismissed." He flung wide his arms. "Forgive and forget, and all that spiritual mumbo jumbo, right?" Revulsion twisted his stomach. When he stepped closer, he knotted his hands, the veins pulsing in his temples. "She broke our marriage vows. She threw away our love. She doesn't get a happily-ever-after. She deserves to rot in hell."

Blinking, Hope stood against his railings. "I'm not saying you both have to reconcile. I'm saying you have to let go of your anger and your disappointment. You have to grieve this loss now, so you don't carry it around as long as you carried the loss of your children." She steeled her gaze. "You are red. You need to be blue."

"Blue?" He tossed back his head and laughed. "What am I?" He tapped his chest. "Some sort of paint-by-numbers the Great Spirit wants to play with?"

She breathed in slowly, unwavering.

Punching a fist into an open palm, he paced back

and forth across the foyer. "She's a flirt. Her dad was a cheater. But I always thought she wouldn't follow in his footsteps." Panting, he stopped and dropped his arms to his sides. "I thought she wouldn't break us." He covered his face with his hands.

Hope took a step forward. "May the Great Spirit be with you, now and forever." She touched his elbow.

The spot on his arm singed with pain, ricocheting through his electrified and raw body. He rubbed his eyes with his fists and heaved a few breaths, blinking several times until he could focus on Hope's stately body standing like a holy statue in an enormous church and asking him to believe in something he had no faith in anymore.

Opening her arms, she welcomed him. "Give me your pain."

He stumbled into her arms, feeling her strength and tenderness envelope him. Closing his eyes, he squeezed out all the bitterness and anger through hot, messy tears. This woman resurrected his sex life with her magic pie. If he listened to her message from the Great Spirit, could he also save his marriage?

****

"Look here." Geraldine leaned against Officer Pollack's rickety desk in the sour-smelling police station. She pointed to the grainy picture on the computer monitor. "Wait for the explosion, then hit Pause, and you'll see his face, bright as day." She leaned back, dropping her arm to her side, and waited.

Officer Pollack slouched near the keyboard, his broad back stretched tight against his uniform. He punched the Play button and squinted at the black-and-white image. A bright light flashed.

"See, here." She leaned over his shoulder and jabbed the screen with an index finger. "That's the arsonist." The monitor showed a man in his late twenties with long black hair swinging in a braid across his shoulders. The man's body partially obscured a sports car in the background. "It's Michelle's boyfriend, Paul. You need to arrest him."

After replaying the scene a second time, Office Pollack wrote some notes. "I'll run the license plate of the vehicle." He stood, motioning Geraldine out of the way. "If the vehicle's stolen, this information won't help us."

Crossing her arms over her chest, Geraldine tapped a foot against the linoleum. Why didn't he believe her? What other man wore his waist-length black hair in a braid and drove a sports car?

A few minutes later, Officer Pollack returned with a sheet of paper. He wriggled his broad nose before he read. "Red sports car belongs to Paul 'Fire Walker' Hughes of the Wapi Reservation." He shook the paper and grimaced. "I'll have to get the tribal police involved."

She sighed. "Why do you guys make everything so complicated?" She threw open her arms. "That man is a criminal. He roughed up his girlfriend, then he came back and tried to take her life." She balled her hands into fists. "How much more evidence do you need before you put him behind bars?"

Officer Pollack set the paper on the desk and folded his arms across his chest. "Mrs. Jones, do I come into the deli and tell you how much mayonnaise to put on my ham-and-cheese sandwich?"

Blinking, she lowered her arms to the sides and

dropped her chin toward her chest. "No, you don't."

"Then please don't come here and tell me how to investigate a crime." He placed a hand on her shoulder and squeezed. "We'll take care of it, just like we took care of those damn kids vandalizing your store last summer."

Breathing in deeply, she loosened her clenched jaw. "Yes, but this situation is different." She swallowed the emotion lodged in her throat.

"I don't see your point." He waved a hand toward the image frozen on the screen. "According to the fire department, no one was hurt."

"But the store was lost." She clutched her fists against her chest. "My whole life was lost."

Officer Pollack bowed his head and sighed. "I'm sorry for your loss, Mrs. Jones." He lifted his head and furrowed his brows. "Don't you have business interruption insurance? You can pay your employees while you rebuild the store. I'm guessing the process shouldn't take more than a year."

One year. Did she want to wait that long? She swept the hair off her hot-and-prickly face.

The phone on the desk rang. "Excuse me." He grabbed the receiver. "Officer Pollack, speaking."

She listened to the drone of his voice as he spoke with the caller, but she didn't register any of the words. Her thoughts were far away and scattered. She hadn't felt so raw since her father died, leaving her and Lionel the store. She remembered him lying on the hospital bed, squeezing her hand and telling her to take care of their employees. "They're family." He blinked his heavy lids and smiled. "Our family." At the funeral, she toyed with the idea of selling the store, abandoning the employee family, and leaving Vine Valley for good. A fresh start. She crossed her arms over her chest and waited.

After hanging up the receiver, Officer Pollack faced her. "I need to get back to work, Mrs. Jones. I'll call you when I have some news, okay?"

She left him her cell phone number, since he could no longer call the store. Outside, in the heat of the afternoon, she squinted and rubbed her cold shoulders against the blazing heat of Indian summer. The sky seemed unusually blue for the season when the light waned, washing out all color. Heavy with foreboding, she opened her car door. She was meeting Lionel at home. They had promised each other they would see the adjuster at the store at three-thirty so he could ask questions and take pictures and finalize their claim. But she didn't feel like she was embarking on another business meeting. She felt like she was attending a funeral.

Chapter Twenty-Four

Sitting in the parked truck beside Geraldine, Lionel felt like he was at a drive-in movie theater, watching an apocalyptic 3-D movie. Wind tunneled through the charred remains of Larry's Deli, blowing bits of debris and ashes like dirty snowflakes across the windshield. None of the fire's aftermath felt real.

"Do you want to walk the site before Brian arrives?" Lionel touched Geraldine's elbow.

Flinching, she blinked away a glassy stare. "I just want to wake from this nightmare." She twisted her hands in her lap.

"I do, too." He leaned back his head and gazed at the two remaining walls facing north and east. Windows were blown out. Glass scattered like crushed ice on the pavement. When he was here last night, he was only concerned about Michelle. Now, gazing at his wife's stoic face, he realized a greater concern. He curled his fingers over her limp hand. "We'll get a quote from Cassidy on the cost to rebuild."

Tugging away her hand, she opened the truck door and stepped outside.

The warmth of her love evaporated, replaced with the chill of her rejection. He trained his gaze on her, wondering what else was wrong.

She ambled up to what used to be the front of the store. The lettering above the door had both *Rs* singed and the *Y* tilted.

He released the seat belt, climbed out of the cab, and approached his wife. The stench of soot and wood clogged his throat, and he covered his mouth and coughed.

"I don't want to be another phoenix." She folded her arms tight against her chest. "Some things should never rise again."

"What do you mean?" He frowned, trying to solve how the riddle fit into this situation. She was always smarter.

"I don't want to rebuild." She kicked at a plank of crisp black wood. After glancing around, she flung open her arms. "Let's sell the land. Retire. Start a new life, either alone or together."

A sudden coldness hit his core. He searched her intent face. She was serious.

"Why keep alive my father's legacy?" She bunched her fists. "We have no children."

"What about our employees?" He took a step closer, glass crunching beneath his feet. "What about the community?" He waved wide his arms.

She scrunched her face and dug her knuckles into her eyes. "We can't—I can't."

The rawness of her emotion forced him to turn away. He couldn't reason with her. She was unreachable right now. He hobbled through the crackle of glass and wood and sat on the bed of the truck, swinging his legs back and forth and waiting for Brian, the insurance adjuster, to arrive. The stink of the burnt remains clogged his lungs, and he coughed, wishing he had a tissue to cover his face. Even his eyes burned. On the wind, the muffled sobs of his wife tightened the hold on his heart. In spite of her indiscretion with Elliot, he could not completely erase her from his life. Too much of his identity was wrapped in hers. He rubbed his face with his hands. But how could he start over when everything they had was lost?

****

Geraldine nodded as Brian spoke, but she wasn't really listening. She focused on his fat lips forming words she would later ask Lionel to translate, her thoughts as untamed as the curling ashes blowing in the wind. Turning away, she strode back to the ruins, avoiding the broken glass and odd nails and splinters of metal jutting from the debris. With her hands tucked in her armpits, she strode along the aisles, remembering where everything used to be. No more fresh loaves of bread and homemade muffins from Sweet and Sassy bakery.

Pinching her nose, she sidestepped the explosion of canned goods attracting a cloud of flies. The stench of death and rotting food stunk in the charred breeze. At the crumbled platform of the deli, she stopped. Like a modern art sculpture, the metal stool curled behind the charred counter. She ran a hand along the sink, leaving the tips of her fingers black. After wiping the smudges on her jeans, she curled her hand into a fist and clutched it against the constant stabbing pain in her chest. Would she ever again make a sandwich that would make a customer smile?

"GG!" Lionel waved. "Brian has a question."

Frowning, she maneuvered her way back toward them, lifting her legs high above twisted metal and charred wood. The stench of the remains tickled her nostrils and stung her eyes. "What do you want to ask?"

She lifted her chin.

Squinting at his clipboard, Brian ticked off the questions Lionel had already answered with his pencil. He hovered above a line. "Do you know when the store was built?"

She struggled to recall the specifics on the deed before she shrugged. "Isn't that information in the public records?"

"I suppose." He lowered the pencil. "I just thought you might know."

Shaking her head, she placed her hands on her waist. "I'm not interested in rebuilding. I want to clean up this mess and sell the property to a new owner."

Brian lifted his eyebrows and glanced at Lionel, who nodded.

Raising her arms, she clutched the sides of her head with her hands. Couldn't they see how difficult this situation was? Why rebuild the place where all of the turmoil of her life originated, from the years working with her father to her pregnancy with the twins to meeting Elliot at the deli counter to the whole debacle with Michelle and her boyfriend? She wanted to leave the past. "I don't want to deal with this paperwork right now." She swiveled toward Lionel. "Handle it. I'll be in the truck." She stalked away, the weak rays of the sun against her back and the strength of the wind before her face. Sitting in the cab, she closed the door and listened to the air hiss through the partially rolled-down windows.

Lionel gesticulated.

Brian wrote.

The pantomime dance gave her the illusion of watching a dark comedy, but the tragedy of the situation lodged in the pit of her stomach, pushing bile against the back of her tongue. Leaning her head against the seat, she closed her eyes and breathed the foul air and wondered if she should also sell the house, leave Vine Valley, and start over where no one knew her name or her history.

But reality shattered her fantasy. Divorce would leave her financially devastated, half of everything being stripped away. Her cost of living would rise with a new mortgage in a new town. She would have to work for someone else. She shuddered. Could she work for someone else? She bit her lower lip. What about Noelle? If Geraldine moved away, would Lionel let her take the dog? If not, how would she feel living without her?

The driver's door creaked.

She opened her eyes.

Lionel slipped inside, the weight of his presence rocking the cab. He shut the door and started the engine. "Brian will get back to us later in the week with some numbers." He drove out of the parking lot and sped down the street. "Do you really want to sell the land?"

Everything about him felt solid and real. She breathed in the lavender soap on his skin. Could she release Lionel, the anchor of her life, and drift from city to city, being a permanent guest? What would happen when she was too old or too sick to travel? Who would care for her like she had cared for her father? Was she prepared to go the distance alone? With a sidelong glance, she shrugged. He had always been her better half—calm, reasonable, grounded. "What do you want?"

Smiling, he flicked his gaze. "I want us to be happy again."

She snickered, shaking her head. "An unlikely story."

"You asked me what I wanted, not what was possible."

"True." The ashes floated away from the windshield, leaving only a gray smudge on the glass. The weight of the fire, the folly of her lust, and the married years of carelessness and neglect fostered by routine and comfort descended on her shoulders. The familiarity of her existence darkened into despair, and she did not know how to exit the pit of her burden to reconstruct a cohesive life.

"So, if we sell the land, do we sell the house, too?" He stopped at a light and met her gaze. "Do we get a divorce?"

A sour taste filled her mouth. She choked on the thought. "Maybe."

Grinding his teeth, he steered onto their street and clicked the garage door opener.

The gaping mouth of their home unsettled her. She gripped the handle on the passenger's side door. "I don't want to go inside." Inside represented the last remnant of their lives together.

"Where do you want to go?" He shifted into Park and let the engine idle.

"Anywhere but here." Her voice sounded small and defeated. She felt like a child, afraid of the dark.

"Here is all we have." He waved toward the open garage.

She blinked. "What about Vegas? We can go to the World Masters next week and get away from it all."

The words rushed out with relief. Any plan was better than no plan.

"I already told Nick I wasn't going."

"Call him and tell him you've changed your mind."

He leaned his forehead on the steering wheel and groaned. "Do you really think a trip to Vegas will save our broken marriage?"

Bowing her head, she clasped her hands in her lap. Why not face the inevitable now? Hadn't she waited long enough? Lifting her chin, she steeled her shoulders. "When do you want me to move out?"

He raised his head and turned to face her.

Oh, why did his brown eyes appear so sad and confused?

"No matter how angry I am with you, I don't want you to move out." He fumbled, searching for her hand. "Please, stay. If we want to continue our marriage, let's start over here."

"I don't know if I want to start over." How could he brush away this pain? She withdrew her cool fingers from his warm hand. How could she trust herself not to make the same mistakes and hurt everyone all over again?

He slapped both hands against the steering wheel. "Damn it, GG. Of course, you don't want to start over. You want to run away." He shut off the engine and released the seat belt. "You were exactly this way after your father died, remember? You wanted us to sell the store and buy a house on the other side of the Wapi Reservation where land was cheap and business was slow. But in the end, we stayed and made the store ours. Not your father's. Ours." Shifting, he held her gaze. "Now you want to sell the land and get a divorce. You think that will magically solve all of our problems. But the store and our marriage didn't cause our problems. You and me, we caused the problems." He waved a hand between them. "We don't just disappear when everything is over. We still have to live with the people we've become and the choices we've made, whether we're together or not." Breathless, he gasped.

The stabbing pain that haunted her all afternoon finally loosened from her chest. She fiddled with the seat belt before pressing the red button. The strap slipped across her body, freeing her to move. She inched closer. The passion in his voice as he had spoken those words resonated like music. She had hurt him irrevocably, and yet he didn't want to get rid of her. He wanted to start over, to rebuild their lives, and to work out things somehow someway. Slowly, she grasped his calloused hands, the hands she had grown to cherish over the years. "Let's go inside. I'll make you a sandwich."

He blinked, tears spilling down his cheeks. "A sandwich will not fix our marriage." Gulping, he squeezed her hands. "I'm moving out. You can stay here with Noelle. We'll need to find a counselor and see if we can repair the damage we've both done."

"A counselor?" Stung by the suggestion, she withdrew her hands. "Where will you go?"

He shrugged. "Nick will take me." Pursing his lips, he spread wide his arms. "I don't want to limp through the next thirty years like we waltzed through the first thirty. I want something sustainable, understand?"

Slumping against the seat, she stared at the gaping mouth of the garage. Two deaths, a pregnant employee, and an out-of-control flirtation led to this crossroads.

After taking a deep breath, she sighed. Being alone would give her time to consider the questions Nick had posed about what was good and what was bad about her marriage. She could decide without interference how she wanted to proceed. Knotting her hands, she wondered what life would look like without Lionel. His presence stretched back as far as she could remember. What would she do without him? What would he do without her? This little separation would answer those questions. Swallowing her uncertainty, she quivered. "I'm scared."

"I am, too." He huffed, pounding a fist against the steering wheel. "I thought we had the perfect marriage."

She grimaced. "Nothing is perfect."

"I know that fact now." He swung open the door and stepped outside. "Are you coming?"

Shaking her head, she waved a hand. "Go ahead and pack."

Standing in a swath of sunlight, he pointed toward the house. "Aren't you making me a sandwich first?"

She twisted her lips into a smile. *A sandwich will not fix our marriage.* But everyone needed to eat. And everyone needed to love. After opening the door, she slipped outside. The warm air caressed her tender skin. With two steps, she met him at the front of the truck. A long shadow of their bodies angled against the concrete—a tangle of arms and legs, discombobulated and wavy, with no beginning and no end.

Thank you for purchasing
this publication of The Wild Rose Press, Inc.

For questions or more information
contact us at
info@thewildrosepress.com.

The Wild Rose Press, Inc.